FROM NOTHING TO SOMETHING

The Power of Obedience

BY RUTH CUBE KEIJDENER

E-book Edition

ISBN ____________________-

THE POWER OF OBEDIENCE

From Nothing to Something

Ruth Cube Keijdener

DEDICATION

Thank You, Daddy God, for this book. It's all for Your Glory.

Honoring my dad: Enrique Cube, and mom: Marieta Cube, for being the best parents.

Honoring my loving husband, Jean Keijdener, for being my ever-faithful lover and supporter.

Honoring my beautiful babies, Edana Joanna and Jana Mckinley. You both are the most ideal babies in this world.

Honoring my powerful family, Yvette, Bong, May, Justin, Jeanine, Jela, Elle, and Isaac.

Honoring my ever faithful assistant, sister and friend Janice and the Beautiful Powerful Women Team.

Honoring the people around the world, who partnered with me in my journey until now.

Thank you lord

ENDORSEMENTS

Rolland Baker

For years, Ruth has been a constant source of sweet, loving encouragement to Heidi and I. Her ministry initiative in Southeast Asia is born out of genuine, fiery zeal that just keeps growing, and I know she will continue to be a precious firebrand for Jesus wherever she is. I commend her for her full-time service in spreading the Gospel and know that her multiple giftings will bear priceless fruit, as the Lord blesses her work and continues to bring life to many through her.

David Hogan

Jesus is King! Ruth is like my daughter. I love, endorse, bless, and back her and her work in the vineyard of our Lord Jesus. She is one of the best Worshipers, Praisers, and Christians I know. I love her as my own.

ABOUT THE AUTHOR

RUTH CUBE KEIJDENER is a Pastor and the founder of Beautiful Powerful Women Ministries and Global Visionary Missions, as well as a film producer of RuachMT19:26 Production PH and a recording artist. While being educated with a degree in Doctor of Optometry, her true calling has been in global missions, healing, and deliverance ministry, in combination with Christian-Events Management and film production. Songwriting, worship leading, preaching, and empowering people are some of her callings. She has an undiluted love for the poor, hence finds them, helps them, and loves on them. Ruth has a long-standing history in traveling the globe for missions and has lived in diverse locations in over 10 countries in the Middle East, Europe,

Asia, and America. Born in Manila, Philippines, she is happily married, for 27 years, to her heartthrob, Dutchman, Jean JK Keijdener, and they have two daughters, Edana and Jana, who are both studying in The Netherlands. Ruth's passion is to let Jesus be known as The Only Way, The Only Truth, and The Only Giver of Life to the ends of the earth.

"God, here is my small life, my small brain, and my small heart.

Make it Your channel, the way it pleases You. Let my life bring Your people closer to You. I desire to partner with what

You are doing, Lord. Here I am, for You."

He simply said, "I love you; you are an obedient child."

"Never doubt God's mighty power to work in you and accomplish all this. He will achieve infinitely more than your greatest request, your most unbelievable dream, and exceed your wildest imagination! He will outdo them all, for His miraculous power constantly energizes you."

TABLE OF CONTENTS

INTRODUCTION

How do you even begin to do something that you have no idea about? Where do you find the courage to do something that you are oblivious about? And how can you put aside your fears and insecurities on doing things that are not your expertise, that you have no experience or knowledge about? What if this very thing is the one thing that God asks you to do for Him?

My stories will surely show you that fear can really be smaller than obedience. That insecurities will surface at some point but will not be able to stop you. That even if you have no resources such as people and material things, it will all be provided to you when you need it. That even if the people you need to work with are not yet in the picture, and you seem clueless about approaching people that seem to be beyond your reach, they will be brought to you with no sweat. You will be unstoppable, even if nobody believes you, or in you. There is always this small, still voice inside your heart and mind that leads you.

I had nothing. I was a nobody. I knew that I was an educated woman, but everything that I did was not in line with what I studied for. I knew that everybody felt that I am lacking and weak.

But I have Jesus.

The author and finisher of my life.

The Maker of all things.

The Creator of the Universe.

The Strength for my weaknesses.

The Joy amidst my sadness and rejections.

My Provider.

He lavishly gave me wisdom with no judgments.

He opens every door for me and talks to every person I need to come to me.

Not because I am special, but because He has a plan and a purpose for everyone, and I happened to say Yes to Him.

I said Yes, because of His love for me.

His love causes me daily to say –

"God, here is my small life, my small brain, my small heart, make it Your channel, the way it pleases You.

Let my life bring Your people closer to You. I desire to partner with what You are doing, Lord.

Here I am, for You."

He simply said, "I love you; you are an obedient child."

God:

Whoever loves Me, obeys Me.

Me:

I will obey, Lord, help me.

God's promise:

I am with you and will walk with you all the days of your life.

Me:

Yes, Lord.

CHAPTER 1
ME GROWING UP

Since I was five years old, I had a very vivid imagination. Unknowingly, I was also very sensitive to the spiritual realm, but instead of being able to use this for good, I felt tormented daily, fearing what I saw. I was paralyzed by torment and fear.

One summer night, I saw ghosts floating around in the room I was staying in at our rest-house in Baguio City. There was a 'Saint Joseph' statue whose head would move and stare at me every time I walked by it in the living room of our main house in Manila. We had a home in the south that had doorknobs that moved in the middle of the night while everyone was asleep. I had nightmares almost every night, wherever I was. On top of carrying the weight of these fears, there was the complexity of growing up in a big family like ours. We were a hyperactive, super-emotional family with siblings who would inevitably fight amidst an environment exposed to guns and drugs. As I was growing up, there were also confusing religious activities that involved rosaries, spiritist4, mediums, horoscopes, and fortune-telling. At one time, we were even baptized as Muslims. Then there was a guest priest who ordained my dad as a cardinal in the new church he felt like he needed to build. We held a new apostolic mass, as he called it, in our home, and also built small churches in our other rest houses.

Nobody knew that all of these intensified the fears I was battling every day. Everyone was busy with their own lives, even though we all lived together under one roof.

My fear of people began when I was a teenager. During those years, I struggled with the pain of rejection. I was confused and wondered why I was always misunderstood; why nobody liked me. All the cutting words and curses thrown at me, by mostly everyone, deepened the pain that I felt and intensified my fear of people. Words and declarations that I was "not beautiful", "always clumsy", "a devil's advocate", "you never finish what you start", or the word, "stupid", stung and totally messed me up. Nothing seemed safe. It was a lot to take in for a young person like me. Life seemed so negative and heavy when all I only wanted was to fit in and be appreciated. I wanted to know my worth as a person, but I had no choice. I felt so trapped.

In those years, even my sleeping pattern was affected. Most of the time, I fell asleep at almost dawn, thinking I'd be safer in the morning when people were already awake. This went on for years. At 16, however, I started to really question life itself.

My parents

My parents were loving and responsible. They were always there for us. Growing up, we had everything we needed, and more. My father was a responsible man, and my mother is very loving. We never ran out of food. There were 10 of us siblings. I had seven siblings from my father's first wife, and I had two siblings with my mother. We were all educated in good schools and finished college with degrees in nursing, dentistry, accounting, optometry, and engineering, to name a few. My mother took care of all of us, and we were all celebrated. Now that I'm a mother myself, I realized that my parents were very misunderstood. But they were actually truly amazing people, and they loved us well in their own way. My father is now in Heaven, but my mother is still alive and amazing, as always. We love her and honor her very much.

CHAPTER 2

SEARCHING FOR A NEW SOMETHING

Looking back, I realized that a lot of the sufferings I went through were instigated by an invisible enemy, but I was oblivious of this. At that time, I did not know anything but fear. Nobody told me that there was an enemy who wants all people completely destroyed, devastated, and dead. The enemy played tricks on me, and for a long time, he won. I believed all his lies and lived under an oppressive fear. So, at sixteen, I wondered if there was another life that was better than mine. Everything just seemed to get worse. I felt trapped, and there was no release.

Religion was introduced to me at a young age, but it just left me confused. However, I knew that there is a God; I just didn't know Him and where He could be found. And then, one night, without even knowing who to call on, I bravely prayed, "If You are real, please take care of me."

The next day, my half-sister brought a Christian pastor to our home. "Jesus wants to take care of you," he said. It made such an impact, for it was the exact answer to my prayer from the night before.

Right there and then, he led me to pray the prayer of accepting Jesus as my Savior and Lord. After that, I went to my room, knelt down, and told God, "If You will love me, I will be Yours forever, and You can send me anywhere."

That night, for the first time in my life, I felt peace. I slept soundly and peacefully, without the nightmares and the terrors. It was amazing! I woke up the next morning feeling refreshed and loved. As far as I could remember, it was the first time I slept so sweetly in the sixteen years of my existence! And the nightmares were gone! I felt like a brand-new person. Indeed, there is a God!

Marked for life

That experience marked me for life. It was the beginning of my "born again" journey. I felt, literally, born again. All of a sudden, I had an identity. I was so filled with love and reassurance that I would never again be alone. I had someone who would walk me through life that I could depend on, and be friends with. I knew then there was a God to follow. There was a God bigger than all my fears, and there was a God whose intention is to fully love me, heal me, and stay with me forever.

I wanted to know everything about God, so I began reading the Bible. The more I read, the more I encountered the love of God. The deeper I tried to get to know Him, the more I fell in love with the God who loved me first. He became a Father to me, the best friend I never had, my comforter, my encourager, my healer, my protector, someone I can belong to. Those are just a few of the things He became to me. I knew then that He is my forever companion. And I loved Him back.

His steadfast love, represented by Jesus Christ, was my main goal. As I read more of His Word, it became so alive within me. There was a specific line that I chose to become my lifestyle. As I read, it was as if He was talking right to me. I heard Him say, "If you love Me, you will obey Me." (John 14:15-17)

Then He also asked me, "Do you love Me?"

I said, "Yes, Lord."

He said, "Feed My people."

Then I responded, "I love You, Lord. Help me obey You all the days of my life. Help me love You. I don't want to live without You."

From that moment onward, I gave Him my total commitment.

Who is God to You?

With a God who loves you intensely, cares about you, saves you, satisfies your heart and wants to give you purpose and identity, would you not obey Him if He asked you to do something?

Would you not want to serve and obey a God who is trustworthy, majestic, and just?

I would.

I've made a decision to obey Him, no matter what. He has become my identity, my main purpose, and my destination. He truly is my life.

CHAPTER 3

A LIFESTYLE OF OBEDIENCE

Obedience is a lifestyle because every day, God will make us decide to obey Him. Obeying Him, however, is such a joy. It's so much fun! He is such a good God, and He makes it all worthwhile. Let me tell you some stories of my daily walks with Jesus, where nobody else is looking, except Him.

In all of my experiences in my daily walks with Jesus, these are my main ingredients:

Love + Faith + Courage + Perseverance.

Love

Love is the universal language that all people can truly understand. So, when He asks me to do something, He wants me to make sure it is all done from love and in love.

Go to the streets and give food

Because of my husband's job, it has become the nature of my family to always move around the world. We get to live in different countries, as the Lord leads us. Our family had just moved to Thailand, when in the first month of settling in, God told me to distribute food to people in the streets. So, I went to the food court at a mall near my house to get what I needed. With packed lunches in tow, I started walking the streets and asked God to tell me along the way who to give it to. Having just arrived in a new country, I didn't yet know their language nor the streets or the rules, but I knew one thing: I heard God, and I just obeyed. He is higher than the law of the land, and love is my license to do his bidding, not just in Thailand but around the world. I saw the faces of the people light up each time I handed food to them, more so as I looked into their eyes and told them that Jesus loved them. When God says, "Go and feed my people", whether there were only two or thousands, our response is to obey. There is no excuse -- not the lack of resources or having just arrived in a new country you have no knowledge about. He will provide for you, and He will make a way for you. As the love of God compels you to do His will in His name, the people you encounter will, in turn, encounter God through you.

Faith

When I hear Him speak and give me instructions, sometimes my logical mind finds it hard to make sense of it, but I still choose to step in faith. That is when I see supernatural things happen, and it causes my faith to increase even more. You will never know the wonderful outcome of what He has asked you to do if you will not take the risk. Isn't it cool? Our faith is strengthened and increased as we go through the adventure of obeying Him. The more risk is taken, the more He shows up. He is such a steadfast and faithful God.

With this story, I encourage you and challenge you to talk to strangers when God leads you to.

I was invited to go to Uganda for a women's conference. I did not think God would say yes and ask me to go.

I said, "I do not think so, Lord, because I don't know anyone there and I have not been there, I also don't know anything about Uganda at all, and my heart has to be right in order for me to go there". My Daddy God, was so patient with me, whatever my thoughts were, but He ultimately knew that I wanted to obey. So, I asked the Lord for a sign if He was really sending me to Uganda. Months passed without a clear answer, so I didn't think about it anymore.

When my family and I went to Europe for a break, I was invited to speak at a church in Belgium. My husband and I were having breakfast at a 5-star hotel the morning I was to go speak at the church when the Lord told me to talk to the lady behind me. I looked and saw a woman who was eating alone. I told my husband to go ahead because I needed to speak to the lady first. My husband knew me so well, so he went ahead.

I went to the lady and told her, "this might sound weird, but the Lord told me to give you a word from Him". She smiled. To cut the story short, all that I prophesied over her, as the Holy Spirit led me, were the exact things she was going through. She was so touched by God at that moment that as her tears fell, she realized that God truly loved her and that He had an amazing purpose for her to be there at that exact time. She told me she had just arrived in Belgium that week to start work. I felt that I had to ask her where she was from originally, and of course, she told me that she was from Uganda. It continues to amaze me that God has such perfect timing and a sense of humor when He confirms things. He used this girl to make sure I knew that I needed to go to Uganda.

You see, if I did not have faith enough to take the risk in order to obey God, I would still be wondering whether or not He wanted me to speak at that conference. He will lead you to the right path and give you specific answers when you seek Him with all your heart and have the willingness to obey Him every time. Faith means taking risks, knowing, with certainty, that He is with you always, ever-present to talk to you, and guide you all the way. Faith also gives you the confidence that He loves you, even if you mess up, and He will always make things work for your good. He will also make sure that your faith will increase, even more, every single time you obey.

Mindset

As we obey God, our desire is that people will also encounter His goodness and His love. Our desire is to be used by the Lord to help others, as we obey Him.

When God asks us to speak to someone, we do not want to feel intimidated, even if we don't know them personally. Sometimes, we may feel that we made a mistake. We may feel that this person is more superior than we are.

When this happens, I go back to the truth that we are all created by one Creator, and we all have needs, strengths, and weaknesses. What God asks us to do may sometimes be hard, or make us feel awkward when we do it, but we have to make sure that His message is communicated across. You don't want to be a hindrance to the amazing revelation and love that God is willing to reveal to a particular person who is going through a specific situation at that point in time. It is always a privilege to obey God when He entrusts us with a message, or to reach the person God wants us to reach. Yes, sometimes, I bargain with God, but I still choose Him. Forget about your fears and go for it.

Here's another crazy story, but with an amazing ending

One night, I was at a round table at a prestigious hotel, with some movie stars, for dinner, when God showed me a vision about the lady in front of me. In my head, I was already telling God, "Please, stop showing me this because I don't think these people are going to listen to me, anyway. Because they are not my circle, and discrimination is probably real with them!" So, I went to the bathroom and discussed more about what I thought with God (He is so merciful and kind and gentle and patient with me), as if my thoughts are better than His, *haha*. He is sooo loving, our Daddy, God.

I was truly being so silly, self-centered, and had the fear of men clearly manifesting in me. But God, in His mercy, knew how to deal with me. He gently and lovingly burned the message in my heart. You see, my intimacy with Jesus looks like this: when I have a Word from the Holy Spirit, and I do not give it to the person, it begins to make me uncomfortable; I felt the burning sensation in my heart. While having dinner, my heart burned the entire time because I kept the word to myself, and I knew that the only way to feel better was to release the message that God had for this woman.

I finally approached the lady and told her what God showed me, and she began to open up to me. She told me that she just found out that her husband was cheating on her, but she trusted God. Throughout her ordeal, we developed an amazing friendship, and I walked with her through some deep pains. While still healing, she got painful news. She had cancer, as well. To cut the long story short, because I said *Yes* to God, she trusted me to pray for her, and she got healed of cancer.

How should our mindset be? No matter how uncomfortable it may be for us, we need to always remember that it is not about us. It is all about God directing you to bless His beloved people.

We need to clearly understand the Love of the Father for His Bride (us), and even if we feel inadequate and uneasy, it will be overruled by the compassion He'll put in our hearts at the end.

Try to think about this: if you obey His prompting, someone may get healed because of your obedience. Through His love and mercy upon us and through us, you get to be the channel of the blessing God has prepared. Oh, what a privilege! It is an honor to truly partner with God.

I ask God to forgive me whenever I get in His way. I ask Him to continue to increase my awareness of His purposes daily and be aligned with Him every single time so that I will obey without question. At the end, I thank God for His never-ending love, partnership, and grace. He gives me new chances every single time.

Perseverance

When the Lord gives me a task, I usually feel that it is too big. I feel that it is too impossible to accomplish, especially by a simple person like me. But then, He will show me the wonderful vision and the fruit of what He is asking me to do: the souls of thousands of people reached for Jesus.

But opposition comes to my front door daily. People can be so blunt in telling you that they don't believe your vision is from the Lord, and they won't give you a chance to explain. They look at your appearance and think that you lack the Holy Spirit. They rudely disagree with your plans, and, straightforwardly, tell you that they are against your cause. They plainly say that you can't do it, or they take your project and make it look like it's their own.

I have experienced this many times, and it's painful. But these experiences have truly made me a better, more loving, and more powerful person. I wouldn't call myself an expert, but the more I was exposed to these circumstances, the more I felt able to receive the grace to forgive, the resolve to continue to love, and the wisdom on how to deal with them in love.

The challenges do not stop there. Sometimes, you don't see things move in the direction you felt led to follow. This happens when it looks like nothing is going right, and your team abandons you, even in the middle of planning.

When this happens, TAKE HEART! God is showing you that you are in the right direction.

Perseverance will lead you to your breakthrough. Fast, pray, and stay humble before the Lord, making sure that your heart is clean and free of anger, bitterness, offense, and all the negative emotions that go with it.

Do you want to know how I do it?

I go to the Lord.

I kneel down on the floor or prostrate myself on the floor with my head faced down.

I put myself in a position of humility before the Lord.

I weep, and I cry before God.

Then, I decide to forgive every single person, renounce the negative emotions, surrender to the Lord every painful feeling and negative thought, and exchange it with peace, love, joy, and encouragement. Exchange the heaviness with His presence, and you will definitely feel better.

When you do this, you win. When you choose love, you always win.

We are not quitters, especially when we know that we are obeying the Lord. We are born with a gift of perseverance in Jesus' name.

This practical story will show you what I mean.

I have been living out of the Philippines for the last 27 years. But

God wanted me to do a two-day conference in Manila, while my family and I resided in Ho Chi Minh, Vietnam. *(This was not the first time I did conferences in Manila, but I will explain further as you read on, and you'll find the connection a little later).*

Through this conference, God showed His power to me in such a profound, redemptive way. He also used this experience of perseverance to heal my heart.

Here we go.

I was never interested in politics

I don't read or watch the news because I found it too negative.

I don't like to be involved with any government-related issues (unless they are geared toward helping the poor).

I did not realize that the pain from my past about my dad and politics was still buried within me. I thought I had already forgiven our government, but when God said to me, "bring my politicians to Me," I was shocked. God asked me to set up a small gathering of politicians alongside the big conference we were organizing in Manila.

He knew my heart so well, including all my sentiments about politics, so I wondered what He was up to. I did not know what to say or even feel, but I knew that God was God, and I could trust Him. I trusted His mandates. He guides me, and I just say, "yes, Lord" all the time! My secret? I know that He will be the one to do it, anyway.

I have zero connections with politicians because I started living abroad as soon as I finished my degree at school. So, that was the first challenge. I was so out of touch. I was completely lost, and some of the people I knew, who had the right connections, did not even want to help me.

Reality hit hard. I felt like Peter when he walked on the water. My eyes and my mind were in the wrong mode now. “I can't do this”, said the voice in my head! Thankfully, the Holy Spirit spoke to me. He reminded me that I don't live in the world’s reality but in the realm of the supernatural signs and wonders of God. I just needed to yield some more, rest more in His love, listen some more, and move forward, even with small steps toward the direction of His vision. Then He will open every door and pour down every supernatural favor to me so that I can complete the journey. Suddenly, I felt excited!

So, in obedience, I went to the hotel, and whether I had someone or not, I booked the function room for the politicians’ meeting, ordered the food, and blocked the date of the event. And as I did that, the journey of favor began.

I got connected to a friend who attended and liked our first conference. She understood my vision and joined our team. She introduced me to a lady who was so sweet and also happened to be the wife of a politician. She told me that I had her full support and she was going to help me. I was so encouraged, but after that meeting, however, I did not hear from her again, nor from anyone in the political scene.

Apparently, it was election time, and politicians do not waste their time with people they don't know. They would not care about people with no renowned names like me. They have no time for any type of invitations as small as mine because they are busy trying to win. I could only say, Help, Lord, Hallelujah!

Yet, I knew that I heard God clearly, and so I was quick to obey without hesitation. God's great glory and strength would have to shine through my weakness again.

I went back home to Vietnam, while my wonderful virtual team led by Janice, my executive assistant and partner, got things done for me.

A month before the conference, I flew back to Manila to do more promotions. However, I got discouraged because people were yet to reply to our invitations.

I barely slept on the flight, but when my plane touched down on Philippine soil, I started praying differently, "Lord, you told me to do this. I am just following Your orders. Did I hear you right?" I asked God to encourage me that day and to show me that He was working with me.

I tell you, when you ask God to show you something, be ready. He is so, so good.

Since I had not slept yet, I chose to go to the spa that morning. I thought to rest there before going to the church later, where I would personally promote the conference.

After a little bit of rest, I went to the church with less than a joyful heart. I was tired, and there were only a few people who registered to attend the conference.

When I arrived at the church, I was called on stage, and though my heart was still heavy, I surrendered everything to the Lord with my hands raised high. Before the service ended, a lady came over and prophesied to me. She said that I was a Daniel and an Esther for the Philippines. I was not very excited about this revelation because, for the last two years, these prophetic words were always declared over me. I heard it too many times, and I felt like it was just another word. After a while, people stood up again for prayer, and this lady approached me again. She said, "I feel like you need to meet the president". I did not want to seem arrogant, but I was not impressed because two years ago, someone already said this to me, but I had not met one politician, and especially not the president. Okay, God, I surrender, and I will let You be God. I truly expected God to move, even though I had no idea about the amazing things He was about to do.

I went straight home and tried to get some rest. But I got a text from the same lady asking me to send her a copy of my passport so that I could get into the Malacanang Palace (white house of the Philippines), to meet the president. I was surprised, yet unsure about it, but I sent her my passport copy, anyway. She texted me back and gave me the time and location that I could meet and pray for the president. Again, in my heart, I was not excited. I decided to wait and see how it would all work out.

But, to cut the story short, praise God because He made it happen. I had the honor of being one of the four people who prayed and prophesied over the president of the Philippines.

Okay, wait, what just happened?

I was so exhilarated. Of course, I was so over the moon!!!

Can you imagine waiting for positive results for months, but to no avail? No one responded to me. Not one politician. Then all of a sudden, the door opened, and the opportunity came for me to pray for the president.

Would that experience not increase your faith? Hallelujah!

I was so blown away! Every time Jesus does something like this, my heart wants to explode with awe and praise. This is the God that I obey!

Jesus and I have this understanding: my capacity and ability are zero, but His is a perfect 10. But He requires my trust and obedience.

Though I wanted to give up, I did not. I chose to persevere. It was only just a month before the conference, and still, the registrations were few. It honestly looked like it was a dead end.

And to top it all, some people said that I used my photos with the president to promote my conference. It felt like an accusation.

How could I use that photo as my promotion? I don't think the president will be pleased. Every single time God does something amazing in my life, I testify about it because I believed in the power of testimony! I wanted people to see that we can trust God to do the impossible for us. If HE did it for me, He will do it for you, too. I use my stories to encourage people. That is my lifestyle.

In the beginning, I did not know anyone, so I rejoiced that God, all of a sudden, in His immeasurable greatness, accomplished what He intended to do in my life.

Please, listen to my heart, as this is the TRUTH that I believe in. When God gives an assignment to all of us, He will provide everything that we need. If the President were required to accomplish what God wanted to happen, He would use him. But I will never dishonor someone. That will forfeit the very purpose of my assignment.

I want people to know God and receive His love for them. You've read my life story. I feel so free now. I feel so loved, and I feel that I have a purpose because of Him. I want all glory to go to God alone.

I persevered and continued to persevere to get God's assignment done for the same reason.

I want you to have what I received.

So, finally, when the day for the politicians' gathering came, I had no idea who would come, but God said to me, "If I can bring you the president, who is the highest authority in the country, will I not be able to help you with the rest of your assignment?" He said to me, "I am the highest authority", and with that, I rested my case.

The room was full of people who needed to be there. A pastor even asked me how I got to invite all of them. But I answered, "I didn't invite them. God brought them to me for His Name's sake."

I blindly and wholeheartedly obeyed God because I trusted His heart and nature. When HE asks me to do something, I do it. I said 'blindly' because I have no idea what our day to day would look like. I may not always be excited to obey at first, especially when my eyes are focused on the reality and not at the vision. But I thank God because His mercy and kindness guide me and lead me back to the right focus, over and over again. What a patient, loving God we serve.

Yes, I choose to persevere. I move toward the vision powerfully through an open communication and intimacy with God.

CHAPTER 4

DREAMS GET BIGGER!

The deeper my love for God is, the more He opens my eyes to see the needs around me, and the more I get stirred up to do more to reach more people. God knows that I truly don't want to waste my time on earth, so I continue to ask Him to tell me how I can be His channel of love and goodness, and how I can serve Him by serving others.

He is so kind to me all the time. He gives me dreams and visions that I know I am not capable of doing all by myself, but HE knows that I will trust Him fully for it.

The more we obey, the more He gives us dreams that are bigger than life.

Our God, as I believe it and as I have continually seen and experienced, is, "The God of the impossible". It is so exciting to live life with Jesus in trust and full obedience.

Let me share with you some of my stories that might encourage you to say yes to God continually despite the process called life, and, of course, if He can do it through me, He can do it through you, too.

Enjoy the journey!

Stay at home mom

Our children were miracle babies. My husband and I knew that we were not going to have children because of some medical condition. But God is the giver of life. In my heart, I knew God would bless us with fruitfulness, and true enough, after 4 years of being married, we had Edana, our first baby. A year and a half later, Jana was born.

There's more to that story, but that will be in another book. For now, God has blessed us with these two joys, and so I have decided that I will be a stay-at-home mom. Plus, when I was growing up, my parents constantly traveled, and I felt like I would not want my kids to experience that, so I never traveled without them for years.

I knew it was my calling to be a global missionary, and it has always been what I wanted to do and what I did before I got married, but when I had children, I chose to be with my family. It was the best decision, and it was worth it.

When my kids turned 13 and 14, God impressed in my heart that it was time for me to start flying again. The kids were, somehow, grown-up, able to take care of themselves, and did not need mommy too much at school anymore.

A few months prior to this prompting, though, I was invited to the very first Christian conference I ever attended. This is where I saw Heidi Baker. I was in an overflow room where I saw her on the screen. But I was so drawn to her, "Wow, Lord!" I thought, "she is speaking my heart. Let me support her, Lord". My lifestyle has always been to look for opportunities to let people know about the love of God. So, in my heart and mind, she was the best to do it for me at this season because she was speaking about what was in my heart about intimacy with the Lord.

A few days later, I was invited to another conference, and this time, it was Bill Johnson speaking, and I felt like, "Wow, he is my kind of guy!" I've been told that I was a bit weird and overboard in how I worship, but here is this man, talking as if he also experienced the same journey and similar manifestations and love of Jesus. I got so thrilled and interested because, more than anything, I was thirsty for God. I was so thirsty and hungry for the move of God.

"Lord, don't let me waste my days. Show me Your move and let me be a part of it". This has always been my secret prayer, but after seeing these two people in two consecutive days, I was so fired up!

I started attending all these conferences in Korea and got so excited because I knew I was finally meeting the people who are supernatural in their thinking. I thought to myself, "I need to be with these people".

My nature and God's divine path

I am considered, by many, to be a radical believer. I would have unusual experiences, and a lot of people often misunderstand me when I share it. Even at church, or especially at church, some people stay away because they don't understand me. I would say that I am not a normal person. I have decided long ago, in my heart, that "I am in the world but not of the world". I am not normal, "I am super-natural". I would go to a different world where I would worship and praise and pray. Ever since I was 16 years old, I have had encounters with God and experienced manifestations of the presence of God, and no one can take that away from me. I have spiritual eyes that people don't understand. Now, after 30 years of being a Christian, I have finally seen people who are like me. So, when God impressed in my heart that it was time for me to start traveling again and make mission trips, I had an in-depth conversation with Him about making the trips with these people. Would that ever happen? I don't know, but there was no harm in asking.

Months passed. My heart was longing for more of God. Then I was introduced to a website called Global Awakening from the Randy Clark Ministry. They invite believers from around the world to travel with them for missions, and at that time, the destination was Taiwan. "Wow," I thought. "Taiwan is not so far from Korea," which was our home base at that time. It was not going to be a long flight. The mission trip was only for five days. After looking more closely, I realized that the trip was going to be with Heidi Baker and Bill Johnson. I was so amazed and excited because this was my exact prayer. This was when I knew that God truly wanted me to start traveling again. It was nicely presented to me on a silver platter. I just knew that it was God, and so, I applied. But I found out very quickly, however, that the application was already closed. I was a week and a half too late. But I did not get disappointed. I decided that since I was going to miss my kids, I won't mind if I couldn't go. At the same time, I decided to send my application still and see if God really wanted me to go. I always believed that no one can shut the door that God opens for me. If it is from God, whether it's a month late, God will make sure it remains open for me. True enough, they wrote back and told me to fill out all the forms so that they can give me an opening.

Just to give you a background on this application. I didn't have the strength to fill out these forms and go through all these legalities, so I asked God to help me. A week before the application deadline, I got a phone call from a friend who told me that she was coming to Korea and needed a place to stay for two weeks. My house is an open house, most of the time, for guests and missionaries, so I invited her in. Little did I know that she would be the one to help me with all my application requirements. She was happy to help, and I did nothing but answer her questions. I sent it and got approved the same week.

The next step was to talk to the kids. I needed to tell them about my trip. I made it into a story that they would understand. I told them how mom and dad started allowing them to sleep over at their classmates' home, when we knew that it was safe, knowing that the sleepover would give them lots of good memories. So, I told them my story, as well. I told them that mommy needed to sleepover, and I asked them to bless me. I explained to them that whatever reward I get because of my obedience to God and the people that I get to bless there, they will receive the same blessings, too, because they allowed me to go. They both agreed with love.

It was the first time I ever left my kids after 14 years of me being with them daily. Call me weak, but it was really hard, and it still is, every time I leave for trips. But the love of God is sufficient to touch our hearts and put it at ease and peace. It turned out to be such a blessing to my family when I was on the mission trip, as the three of them became so closely bonded together when "there was no mommy to supervise." Daddy had to step up and enjoy being the "run-to parent" for the kids' needs, and they had lots of fun, as well. I realized that as we follow God, He takes care of everyone close to us, who might be affected because of our obedience.

I finally flew to Taiwan. Bill, Randy, and Heidi were the speakers, and I had the best time of my life. I was named "ghostbuster" because I used to be sent to the deliverance room, and I would sing over the people who had some different types of spirits, and they got delivered when I sang over them.

On the last day of the conference, God acknowledged my awakened desire to organize such powerful and purposeful Holy Spirit-led conferences. I totally loved the idea of organizing a conference like that. It totally changed me, and I wanted to tell others about it, but I brushed it off, thinking that it was too impossible, too big, and I had no idea how to do it. I didn't even know the people who could speak at these conferences. I went home, and life went on. I set aside the dream and vision and just continued my everyday life of sharing the Gospel in every way I could to whoever I could share it to.

A few months later, it was my family's time to move again. We had dearly enjoyed our time in Korea, but we had to move every 5 years or less. However, I asked God not to bring me back to developing countries for a while because it broke my heart seeing beggars, drug addicts in the streets, prostitutes, and homeless people. It hurts me too much when I can't do anything for them.

At that time, we had two places to consider, Japan and Thailand. I prayed for the obvious. We've traveled and had so many vacations in Japan. We loved every bit of it, and I have not seen one poor person there.

Don't get me wrong; even if I have a very comfortable life, I never stop looking for people to help. Truly, God knows that my heart is totally for Him, and my desire was to be used for His glory, as His hands, feet, and heart. In every country we go to, I pray that God will send us His people and send us people to help, especially missionaries. I poured God's love on them and tried to provide for them, even shelter when needed. My heart's desire is just to help in the humblest way possible. Plus, I have always made myself available for "inner healing and spiritual counseling", which has been my ministry for the longest time. I live daily with a mission to reach souls so that they can receive a love encounter from Jesus.

But I thought that moving to Japan would be an easier transition for my family. I thought that life there would be as comfortable as our lives in Korea. The style of living, amazing cleanliness, super yummy food, exquisite culture, and the nice weather was so inviting, and my heart would not break seeing poor people on the streets. I felt confident that God would bring me to the place I thought was best for me. I chose Japan, but God had another plan. He chose Thailand. I couldn't do anything about it anymore, so I prayed, "If you will not do greater and bigger things, though, please don't bring me there. I am almost 43 years old. Lord, I want to do more for You. Have Your way."

My lifestyle is one of obedience, so if He says, "Go to the people", I go: whenever I can, whoever I meet or even sit with, in cars, streets, airplanes, hotels, or malls. If God tells me to talk to them, bless them, pray for them, feed them, heal them, I would. But this time, my heart was drawn to dream bigger. How do I reach tens of thousands and millions of people? This time, I boldly asked God for a massive movement that would glorify Him. It led me back to the vision and dream that I had in Taiwan. Even before we arrived in Thailand, I knew I would be doing a conference just like the one I attended in Taiwan.

We made a short visit to Bangkok to see how it would be there for us as a family. Straight away, God gripped my heart with compassion as I walked the streets of Bangkok again. It is so different when you go to a place for a vacation than when you are about to live there. He showed me, in a vision that seemed like a movie, the things that broke His heart. I vividly remember that I started sobbing in the middle of what He showed me because the pain was so intense, I could not take it. My heart was convinced that I had to do something. I cried so hard. The very thing I did not want to see was right before my eyes, HE showed me, though it broke His heart first. I started dreaming big, only because the need seemed immeasurable for me.

The need was so vast that I thought reinforcements were needed from the family of believers outside the country. Thailand was such a beautiful country, and every race seemed to be represented there. That is how Revive Asia was birthed in my heart. *We are in Asia, Lord, revive us.* That was my heart's cry. Revive us here in Asia, Lord. Revive Asia.

CHAPTER 5
REVIVE ASIA

A month after arriving in Thailand, I started to ask Him to lead me and show me what to do so that I could partner with Him for His plans. I was aware that this country tolerates every type of spiritual activity, but I also knew that the love of God and His blessings are in abundance for this nation. In my first week in Thailand, I already faced discrimination and opposition, so I thought, "okay, I'm on the right track. Jesus, help."

I knew that I was coming to a new territory. I knew I would be doing something truly impossible, so I needed to be sure that what I was set to do did not just come from my compassion, but from God's heart for the people.

I started meeting with a lot of missionaries and leaders who have been assigned there or were working there. Their joy was so depleted that they'd ask me, at some point, why I was so joyful. My heart broke so much. I knew that God wanted a revival to happen in this land. Because I am in Asia, the conference name "REVIVE ASIA" will be appropriate.

So, I started to prepare. From the first week, there was already too much opposition. But this assignment burned greater than anything in my heart. I felt so much love and compassion for the people that I knew, straight away, there had to be a revival in the very heart of Thailand. Reinforcements from the family of believers from around the world were needed. The fire of God, the love of God, the hope from God, the joy of God, and His very Presence has to be encountered by us all where we are, so I, again, said, "Yes, Lord, let's Revive Asia".

So many thoughts would rush into my mind daily, including the reality that I was new in Thailand, that I didn't have any home church yet, that I did not have anyone close to me yet that would capture my vision, that I did not know who to approach. There were also a lot of personal attacks from the people in the hotel where we lived, which was also my husband's workplace. So, I quickly asked God, "Can I do this, God?"

Thankfully, my kids were already grown up and were able to explore high school and their new world on their own. My hubby was already busy with work from day one. I was alone at our place most days and kept asking God for signs and directions.

A few months after arriving in Thailand, we had to go to Europe for a family visit, but I felt like I needed to also go to a conference an hour away from our place. My very supportive husband brought me there.

While there, I would ask God every day to show me a sign that would gear toward Revive Asia, and I would be so amazed at how He answered me every single time.

I remember in one session of the two-day conference, I told God,

"Lord, I think I am afraid to do the Revive Asia Conference." Although it started to become truly apparent that God was calling me to do it, it also started to dawn on me how vast a conference it would be, like the one I was attending in the Netherlands, and I have no idea how to manage it or make it happen. I have never done anything this before. I also did not have the funds for it. Funny enough, while the speaker was praying, he laid his hand on my head and started shouting, "Courage! Courage! Courage!".

What really sealed the deal for me, that caused me to be so sure about my up and coming assignment in Thailand, was the events that happened on the last day of the conference. I said, "God, if I get to hug Lauren Cunningham, the founder of YWAM, then I know for sure that You are talking to me."

Let me give you a short backstory.

The day before that, Lauren Cunningham spoke at the conference more than once, but right after his session, he was nowhere to be found. I figured that the next day he would be out of sight again, so it will actually be a miracle to even talk to him. That was just my small mind, thinking. My doubts were sometimes silly, and I had to ask God to confirm this assignment to me by giving me the opportunity to hug Lauren (yes, I am a hugger). So, that day, he announced that after his session, he would do a book signing. I thought, "Oh my, of all days!" So, I came to his table without a book, and I just looked at him and asked him, "Do you think I can hug you?" He said, "Sure". He opened the small door between us so that I could get through to him. I hugged him, and he then said to me, "I NEEDED THAT!" Then I heard God say that He needed me to do the Revive Asia conference for His glory and the good of His people. I knew then that it was a mandate directly from Heaven. Not just by compassion anymore, but by obedience. It was God I heard, and the vision was on point. The signs asked were given, now it was time to roll.

The vacation ended, and we went back home.

Everyone, except me, went back to their usual routine. Something changed in my heart. I became intentional and focused with my moves and my decisions. This is because I never take lightly the assignment that God gives me. Only by His grace can an impossible mission be accomplished. I had mixed emotions.

God gave me four visions for four consecutive years of the Revive Asia conference. After arriving from Europe, I still did not have any leads or resources to start anything. I just kept praying and waiting. "How, Lord? Who do you want me to work with, and who can I partner with?"

One day, I was lying on my bed when God brought me into a trance. I saw a vision of a stage. I knew exactly where that stage was. It was a stage in one of the churches I visited before.

I started attending that church again since the Lord showed it to me in a vision. After a few months of going there, I asked for an appointment with the pastor. The first thing I told Him was, "I have a mandate from the Lord, and his church is part of it. Let's do Revive

Asia Conference". He was shocked, and he told me, maybe I could be a connector for his church. I said, "Great!"'. That was a good start.

I have not heard from him for a long while, so I made an appointment again. I was so bold because I knew God commissioned me to work with him. We met again, and this time, I told him what God told me about what was happening in his church. I hoped he would realize that I was truly hearing from the Lord. Again, I told him that God gave me the heart to revive Asia, and He wanted me to partner with him. But he was not convinced.

Although I kept on telling the pastor that I will bring Heidi Baker, Randy Clark, and Bill Johnson, as the conference speakers, to Revive Asia, I had not asked any of them yet. But somehow, I had so much peace that God will let them come to me. I did not have a close relationship with any of them yet, at that time.

Amid everything that I was doing in Thailand, I felt I needed to be refreshed. I was involved with so many organizations, prayer, and inner healing ministries, and anti-human trafficking organizations. I did prison visits, prayed for, and helped women and leaders because the needs were so much. So, I traveled in and out of the country, attending conferences, mission trips, and other personal trips. Through it all, Revive Asia was burning in my heart more and more. Oh, Lord, lead me.

How do I get the speakers, Lord?

I flew to Singapore for a conference for a few days with the intention of resting. I also needed to connect with Heidi, Randy, and Bill to finally invite them for Revive Asia. They still had no clue about it, and they didn't fully know me yet at that time. As soon as I got there, though, I couldn't see any opportunity to approach them.

I prayed.

“Lord, if I won't be a part of the ministering team here, I will not have access to Your people, so let me know if I need to stay.” Before I left that evening, the head of Global Awakening, whom I traveled with in Taiwan, saw me. He did not ask me if I wanted to help them out with the ministering team, he just told me, “Ruth, good to see you here. I will give you your ID tomorrow to help us minister.” It was perfect. That meant that I would have backstage access, which will give me the opportunity to approach the speakers and invite them to Revive Asia. I also wanted to ask Randy for an impartation because my heart truly needed it.

At the end of the conference, before Randy went home, I told him, “It's time to go to Bangkok.” He looked at me and said, “Okay, tell Paul (his assistant).” I went to Paul and got connected to him. I knew I got Randy already. Thank You, God; how about Heidi and Bill?

Papa Bill and Mama Heidi

After I saw Papa Bill in Korea, I made sure to attend Bethel Church in Redding with my family whenever we visited my parents and siblings in America. That was when Bethel was just starting, and they were not so well known yet, but I would go there, knowing that we experienced the same encounters with God. We would see Bill's family at church, but there was no personal contact with them.

So, I just believed in my heart that God would bring them all to Revive Asia since it was His idea.

Fast forward, two weeks prior to me flying to Singapore for the same conference as Randy and Heidi, I prayed, "Lord, can You please embrace me, sing over me and tell me something nice and sweet to encourage me." At that time, I was doing a lot of ministering in Thailand and felt the need to be filled and refreshed by God. When I flew to Singapore, I forgot all about this prayer until the night that Mama Heidi preached about it in Singapore. In the audience, I stood beside Papa Bill, and Mama Heidi said, "Embrace the person beside you and say Hi." Papa Bill was beside me, so he hugged me (I felt the Father's embrace). While he hugged me, he started to hum a song over me, and after a few minutes, he looked at me and told me, "You are an obedient child". I cried buckets because God spoke to me through that encounter. He answered my request for a hug, sang over me through Papa Bill, and told me something nice to encourage me. The very words he spoke, "You are an obedient child" were the exact words my dad told me when I was young, so I knew it was such a kiss from Heaven. I somehow managed to tell him that it was time for him to come to Bangkok. He just said, "Really?" I said, "Yes!" and that was it; no formalities, no exchange. He did not tell me to talk to his secretary or something, but because of my encounter with God, I was so encouraged and really knew deep within that God will make a way.

I went back home to Thailand, so fired up and full again. Immediately, I asked for another appointment with the pastor. I said that I had a mandate from the Lord, and he was in it. Then he finally said, "Actually, I have a domain name called Revival Asia or something like that for a while now", so I said to him, "That is even better; it's a confirmation, so let's partner in this together." I felt like he was not as keen as I was. I knew that he saw the fire in my heart already, but still, nothing.

I flew to Manila because I connected Mama Heidi there for a conference. There was a lady who was so angry with me because Mama came with me instead of her, but I told her that I would let her have time with Mama Heidi on her own. Because time was short and the schedule was hectic, I could not find the chance to talk to Mama Heidi properly on my own. The lady also kept on planning things for me to do and kept me so far away from Mama Heidi, so I just prayed.

"Lord, open up the door for our meeting because Mama Heidi is already leaving tonight." As soon as I finished that short but precise prayer, I went to the elevator to go down for the lunch break, and as soon as it opened, there she was. She blurted and said, "Ruth, Rolland, and I need to talk to you about Bangkok." I said, "I needed to talk to you about Bangkok, too." So, we agreed to meet at the restaurant while she rushed back to her room to get something. When I arrived at the restaurant, the lady was there and asked me, "why are you here?". She was clearly upset. "I bumped into Mama Heidi, and she told me to come here," I answered. I knew she didn't want me there, so before she could ask me to leave, I said, "But you know what, just please tell her that I came by, but I will just have lunch with my brother in law", and I left.

One thing I learned in the years of ministry is that it's not the people you need. It's Jesus. There are things in your life you have no control over, and all of us can say that. So, whoever you will need, pray about it. Don't stop trying, but keep pushing, because He Himself will provide what you need, and He will not allow people to come in between. I left Manila and went back home without seeing Mama Heidi again. But I was so full of hope.

But glory to God, Mama Heidi contacted me. She said God told her to ask me to help organize their Iris Ministries family gathering in Thailand. I did my best to organize it, and everyone was happy with the event. On our last day, I finally had time to ask her, in the hallway, if she would be my guest for the Revive Asia conference, and she said yes. Then I asked her if she could invite Papa Bill also for me because my timeline was getting shorter, and I needed her help. She said to me, "Oh, perfect, I will have lunch with him the day after I arrive in Redding, I will let him know." She asked me for some more details, and after a week, I got the three of them confirmed as speakers for the Revive Asia Conference. That is just Jesus.

I was so excited because now I had the three powerful speakers that are not easy to book, but I believe that God used simple vessels like me to achieve powerful things.

Moving on with the conference, I felt in my heart that there must be a representative in Asia, so I invited a Pastor from the Philippines, and I also invited Jake Hamilton to do the worship. The team was complete, and with God's help, I had done my part with setting it up.

When we carry the mandate of the Lord, we cannot be denied by anyone. So, finally, the pastor in Thailand agreed to be part of the conference.

Next, I needed to think about the venue.

Excellence for the Lord is a must.

This conference must be held in the heart of Bangkok, at least, that is what I thought. Amazingly, the Vice President of the organization that owned the biggest convention center in Bangkok was our family friend, and so I asked him to connect me to the people there. He said to me, "Ruth, don't expect them to give you a discount, okay?" But I told him, "don't worry, Jesus will be the one to give us the discount."

I got a phone call from the people in the church that I partnered with that they already went to the venue without me, and they got a 10% discount. I was disappointed that they do things without me when in fact its supposed to be a partnership, but I chose to look at

Jesus. I told them to meet me there and wait for me to speak to the people in charge. I felt that because God called me to arrange this conference, then His favor will fall on me. So, we set the appointment to meet the two ladies in charge of the venue.

I always give people the opportunity to be loved by Jesus first. When we are given a mandate by the Lord, don't ignore the people that He brings to you, for they are also your assignment.

At the meeting, God gave me a word for the ladies. I prophesied over them just as the Holy Spirit led me to. I prayed for them, and they felt so loved by the Lord. They were so touched that they cried. When we finally talked about the arrangements, we ended up getting a 28.5% discount and lots and lots of leeway for all our demands. You have to understand, though, that this place is packed two years in advance because this is the only convention center that is in the middle of town, so it was not normal to be given a huge discount. But I told you, Jesus will!!!

So many more miracles happened during the preparations for the event, although there were also some conflicts and misunderstandings. But I still was able to focus on the vision and walk in honor, even if the people around me did not honor me.

One thing I want to highlight is this: after the event, the pastor of the church told me that my reward is full in Heaven because nobody knew what I had done. I was nicely hidden. There was no mention of my name, no acknowledgment or thank you was given to me. I will admit that I was a little hurt, not because of the lack of recognition, but because I couldn't believe that thanklessness could exist within the family of believers.

My obedience, however, is solid with Jesus, and my focus was on the people. Through His mercy, no hurts or disappointments will stop me from doing what He wanted me to do, even if it became so painful. During the Revive Asia conference, I saw how participants, who traveled from all around the world were able to unite and receive so much fire and awakening from the Holy Spirit. With or without recognition, the very mandate that God gave me was to organize this conference with this church and seeing it fulfilled is just the best thing. The Holy Spirit showed up, and revival happened.

Despite being hidden, I did not stop. God gave four Revive Asia conference projects for four years. I asked God if I was to work with the same pastor again, and He said YES. So, for three more conferences, I did what I needed to do to invite speakers and help organize the speakers and do what I needed to do . I did not demand anything, I just worked for Jesus, but on the fourth one, Jesus said, "No more!"

My reason for writing this story is to point out that surely in our life's journey, whether it be at work, in our family, or ministry -- offenses, dishonor, opposition, disgust, and frustrations are inevitable. Admittedly, it is hard to obey what God is asking from us when we have to deal with these. I want to encourage you, though, that it is possible to put God above all disappointments and hurts. I went through it every single time, and I came out clean.

How? By being so broken and open and surrendered to the Lord.

Whenever I was offended, I would seek out God and ask Him to change my offended heart into a clean and holy heart. This is because I want to see God the way He is and not through my eyes, blinded with pain or offense or frustration. Obedience enables us to forgive, bless others, and let God handle the people we encounter. We just have to follow His leading. His love will always heal us along the way if we are willing.

Our eyes have to be focused on Him and not on what people do to us. Our expectations are supposed to be focused on God and not on the people.

Obedience means forgiving every minute, if you must, to make sure there is no open door for deception and tainted visions. We want our hearts to be clean so that the love of God can flow through us to others and bring them life. We need to forgive in order to be set free from the repercussions of wrong decisions and be able to move in joy, as we continue to obey.

When our heart is free, we can honor people, even if they do not reciprocate it. It is such a privilege to be like Jesus, loving and honoring people, even if they don't deserve it. Obedience lets you experience all these and more.

CHAPTER 6

BETHEL WORSHIP

After the events, and after experiencing pain and forgiveness, after witnessing the amazing miracles, and learning lessons on partnering with a church, God told me to do something else. This time, it was to be on my own. So, I started dreaming with Him again, asking Him what was next.

While praying, it came to mind about bringing Presence-filled worship. I know the transformation worship brings and that was the only one left that I have not done yet in Thailand. I asked God for them to come to Thailand. Their worship songs were such hits all over the world, too. I wanted to bring them in, so I wrote to them. But I got no response.

I started to cast this vision to some famous people that attended the Revive Asia conference. Some of them knew me, so I thought that they would capture what was in my heart, but there were too many excuses, and few of them bluntly said that they don't think I could do it.

Since Bethel did not respond, I said to God, "Okay, God, I tried, I'm available and will just wait for You." I said to Jesus, "Unless they call me on the phone, I will not beg them, but if You want this, God, I will be ready." I also decided right there and then that I didn't have to mind people's opinions about me -- that I can't do this project because I was an unknown, that I can't do it because I have no church and supporters, no ministry partners and no resources.

To the world, doing this alone, given my limitations, might be foolishness, for sure, and in reality -- it probably lacked common sense, as well. What they did not understand is that, though I am in the world, I am not of the world. I have a God, who is the source of everything, He has a plan, and I'm in it for the good of His people. He is my Father, and I get my assignment from Him. So, I know it will be done, just not at the time that I expected. I will just wait for Him.

You see, you need to make sure it is God you heard from so that, even if people look down on you and be rude to you, and belittle the vision God gave you, you can go on and not lose focus. Just continue loving.

By then, I have not heard back from Bethel Worship for a whole year after I contacted them. What a surprise when, just as I was preparing to go for my mission trip to Manila, Philippines, I got a shocking phone call from Singapore, telling me simply, "Bethel is coming to Thailand. Would you like to host them?"

The thing is, why would Bethel call me? First and foremost, I am not a Thai person. Personally, they had no clue who I was. My mind was set that I will just do what God asks of me, and I didn't need any titles or names, so I did not care much for that until I was told I needed to create one.

When the man who called me started to explain what they wanted and needed, I told him the truth, that I had no support from anyone yet, not even a church, but if they will believe in me, God will help me make it happen because He promised me He would bring Bethel Worship to Thailand through me. And he said, "Okay."

My mind started to whirl like a tornado, right away. "Okay, God, You know already that I have no team. I have no music company to bring in a full-sized 22-24-piece band with all of their instruments. I don't even understand their terminologies, and I don't have a job to finance me," I told Him.

I fell prostrate on the floor and prayed to my Almighty, all-knowing, powerful, invisible, miracle-working God. I will obey and believe.

I knew, with all my heart, that miracles upon miracles are expected to happen, but I was daily on my knees. I quickly called my friend and told her everything.

First things first, I thought, "Where would the finances come from for this worship concert because I will be needing this much (I quickly calculated), and I don't know anyone who can help me?"

But just as I came out of my room, a random lady called me and said, "I want to give you financial support because I heard from my friend you are going to host Bethel Worship and I love them". She gave me 10% of the projected need as if she was there in my room, listening to my prayer. The thing is, she did not even know me. I told her that just in case it doesn't push through (since that was the first day after I got the phone call from Bethel), I will give her back every cent she gave me for it. But wow, that encouraged me big time.

The reality also hit me that I only had 5 weeks to get this done. To top it all, I had no team, and I was going to the Philippines for missions. Well, God stretches time; I just needed to do what I could and believe that He would help me all the way just like before.

Who will join me in this project?

Praise God. Since I do a lot of inner healing and deliverance ministries, I recently met up with this young American Thai girl in her 20's, who just moved to Thailand. She needed someone to be with her all the time, and I treated her like my own daughter. I told her I have this vision , if she is willing to help me . She said yes.

Then I got a phone call from another girl whom I met in the Netherlands that summer a few months back, and she said she was in Thailand for a while, and if there was something she could help me with, she would be willing to do so. She also said that she'd pull in her brother to help. I also had a young guy friend whom I took in as a family member while I lived there. He was very creative, and he was also willing to help. To complete my team, I needed someone connected to the entertainment industry who could help get the band in the country to perform. Thankfully, before all of these, I met someone in the music world, we worked for my music before. He was an English guy married to a Thai lady. He knew exactly what I did not know. So, within a week, my team was complete. There were five of us to take care of twenty-four people, which was just right. I knew the angels and heavenly hosts would cover all our other needs. Hallelujah!

Major needs

There were 3 major things that were crucial and most difficult to solve that I needed to pay attention to first. After that, I believed the rest would just fall into place: accommodations of the guests, venue for the worship, and marketing strategies.

Bethel Worship was not popular at all in Thailand at that time, but I needed to sell tickets to cover their costs, and I wanted to make sure that there was enough for their honorarium.

God is sovereign; He sees the big picture!

Six months before I received that call from Bethel Worship, I felt like God was telling me to pray for someone in the hospital. I thought, "Okay, God, which hospital? Where? How do I know who to pray for? Just let me know, God." I didn't get an answer and forgot about it after a few days.

I called a friend because I felt like having high tea one day and asked her to come with me, but she declined because she had to go to the hospital. I got so excited because I remembered God told me to pray for someone in the hospital. I almost screamed, "Can I come?" and she said, "Yes. Come with me."

In the hospital, I was so drawn to a lady that was in a coma in the ICU. I just felt so much love for this lady. I knew that God gave me the privilege and honor to love her so that I could passionately pray for her.

I asked my friend if I could visit the lady in the hospital every day, even though her family was not there, and they did not know me. She said yes.

I went every week, and finally, I met the lady's daughter. I didn't know who they were, I didn't even know where they came from, I didn't know what their background was, but it did not matter to me because I was excited that the Lord asked me to pray for someone in the hospital. I heard Him so well, and it was a pleasure to pray for her.

I loved my time with the daughter. We exchanged stories. I encouraged her; she encouraged me, too. We prayed and worshipped every time. I made sure I whispered to her mom's ear, Mama Joyful (different name), "You will open your eyes. You're gonna wake up, and we're going to have tea together." It went on like that for a month or more. I visited often, and eventually, I met the entire family. I was able to pray with the lady's brother, her husband, and her son. We became like family.

During the winter break, I needed to fly with my family to America for a vacation, so I told Mama Joyful that when I come back, her eyes would already be opened. Wherever I was, and whenever I remembered her, I would pray and declare life to her. I, literally, would open my mouth and say, "Wake up, Mama Joyful," as if I was beside her. I did this until the time I returned to Thailand, and by God's grace and mercy, her eyes were already opened when I visited her.

Why am I telling you this story? It's because, apparently, the daughter's husband is the CEO of a group of prestigious five-star hotels around the world, and they had a lot of hotels in Thailand. When I needed hotel rooms for the Bethel group, I called her and requested if she could ask her husband for a good discount. She said she would not only ask her husband for a good discount, but she would also pay for all the rooms. Now, that is Jesus. All of a sudden, the hotel rooms I needed were fully paid for. I only had to take care of the food for the band, and for that, they gave me a 50% discount. Glory to God!

I want you to understand that I did not pray for the mom to get something from them. I prayed for her because I heard God say He wanted me to pray. Through my friend, God brought me to the person I was to pray for. Did you notice I was always ready? I obeyed, and without my knowledge, He orchestrated it all for His purpose. The worship concert was His event for His people.

We sometimes wonder why we should obey, but God always saw the bigger picture and has everything all planned out so nicely for us. It will, in the end, turn out to be such a beautiful story, even if it was not pleasant at the moment. Let's trust God and obey!

With or without resources, with or without help from others, I strive to move forward with the vision that God gives to me, knowing that God sees the big picture, and His nature is faithfulness.

My desire for unity Got me the concert hall

As soon as I finished partnering with the previous church, I felt a nudge from the Holy Spirit, to invite and host 50 local pastors to the hotel where my husband worked. I set up a nice luncheon for them and organized a program that I hoped would break the walls of disunity and encourage them to work together in love. That was the clear mandate for that event. It was such a successful endeavor because they started to talk to each other again, and they did not even want to go home. They had so much joy; it was such a delight that I also had an opportunity to get to know them. I was invited to lead worship at one of the local churches, as well.

I got to speak with one of the local pastors, who attended that lunch and told her my desire to bring Bethel Worship to Thailand. I told her I needed some help. She introduced me to another pastor she knew, whose daughter actually studied at the Bethel School of Supernatural Ministry (BSSM).

I went to see him. He was so pleased to find out that I was the one who hosted the luncheon for the pastors. I told him about bringing Bethel Worship to Thailand, and he informed me that they have been trying to invite them, but only the BSSM students came. Then I asked him if he would be interested in partnering with us. I told him what we needed about the venue for the concert. He said that his church would cover 90% of the funds required, and all I needed to secure was the remaining 10%. I was so relieved. The venue was paid for! That is Jesus.

Thankful for the known artists that the crowd does not recognize

There are still people who do not understand that there are always costs involved in organizing events. I know some people cringe when we talk about Christianity and expenses at the same time, but all events had expenses. And there were still some costs that would have to be paid through the ticket sales. We had to generate funds through ticket sales, even if Thailand did not really know who Bethel Worship was. We had to take the risk and sell.

I asked God for a strategy, and He gave me a simple one. He told me to reach out to my friends and let them sponsor the people who will come. I started telling some of my friends abroad to sponsor some tickets because people here did not understand yet the effect of what we are about doing. I could only reach a few, but they did sponsor tickets. Then the guy who was from the entertainment business told me about his friend, who was a ticket master. He helped us market tickets with a commission, and even though Bethel was not popular yet in Thailand at that time, the place was packed. The tickets were sold out.

As we obey God, He strengthens us and encourages us. He shows us His love through the small and big miracles we experience along the way.

Highlights of my personal encounters

When the Bethel Worship band arrived, I wanted them to understand why they were in Thailand, even though they would only sing for one night. But they arrived in the evening, and I did not find the time to talk to them about this. We gave them a welcome dinner and introduced them to the sponsors, and then they had to go to their room and rest. The next day after breakfast, Brian Johnson and his son came down and said they needed to go shopping, so I drove them to the mall. While we were driving, I told them about my heart for Thailand and why I thought God brought them there, and so he asked me to lead their devotions that night before they had to go on stage. A small, tiny, little Filipina, will lead a devotion for the number one worship band in the world? That was a humbling moment for me. That was a kiss from Heaven.

Another highlight for me was the time I spent with Bethel singer, Amanda Cooke. She informed me that when she goes to Asia, there will be an Asian woman who is like a lion and child-like in character that will give her a word from God. She approached me for prayer and asked me for that word. Why was that special to me? By that time, their group had already traveled to 5 different Asian countries, but she did not find that one lion and child-like woman in those places until she came to Thailand, and God told her that it was me. That was another humbling moment for me - another kiss from Heaven.

The worship event was successful. The people worshipped, and God was glorified.

Also, God vindicated me in style, even though that was not my focus or desire, but it was so sweet for God to have done it for me.

Everybody wondered how I could pull it all off when they doubted that I could do it. All of a sudden, they wanted to be my friend. But it was all Jesus. I made sure that my heart remained pure in the Lord. Clear of offense and full of love.

The promptings in our hearts that God puts there, our conversations with Jesus and our desire to take part in His move will not make sense to a lot of people and even to us, sometimes. We can get overwhelmed and be convinced that the task is not doable, but as we choose to step up in obedience, move in faith, take risks and trust Him, He will see us through every step of the way. He will even vindicate us in every way possible with style.

When I start doing something for God, I get this vision of myself standing in front of this very high beautiful mountain. And I needed to climb it to get to the other side. In this vision, I climbed the mountain with Him all the way. We talk, we cry, we rest, and we take one step at a time. It started with a vision and a desire to bless people. At the end, it brought me life and joy and increased my faith. He is worthy of my praise, adoration, affection and total devotion.

He increases our faith for yet, bigger and larger things.

CHAPTER 7

BEAUTIFUL POWERFUL WOMEN MINISTRIES

My husband and I felt like it was time for us to move because we were becoming empty-nesters already. Our first child was now settled for a year in her university in the Netherlands, taking up a course on international law. Our youngest child just finished her high school in Thailand and, like her sister, has also decided to study in the Netherlands, on a fine arts degree, majoring in photography. We both love them so much, and we fully support their every move. In our heart of hearts, we knew that the four us had to release each other to the Lord and trust Him to fill us with hope, peace, and joy through the pain of being away from each other for the first time. Oh, my goodness, it was hard!

My husband and I also knew that we had to start asking God where we should go and what we should do in our new season as a couple. Our 18 and 20-year-olds are both now on their own and could take care of themselves, not needing dad and mom for their immediate needs. Whenever we had to move, we had to always consider what country to go to because of their schooling. They were always the first priority. But now, it was a completely different ball game.

We resigned, as we felt like it was finally time to move out of Thailand. This will be the very first time my husband will have a longer break, and we decided to take it easy. We thought, "Okay, God, show us what is next, and where do You want us to be."

We all went to the Netherlands after our youngest child's graduation to ensure that they are settled there. My husband and I decided to travel a little bit more.

We went to so many places, but deep within, my heart was burning for His direction. I kept asking the Lord what was next after Bethel Worship.

Due to our tight schedule, I could not remember exactly which country I was in when I got the revelation from God. We went from one country to another, but I think I was either in Turkey or Prague when I got an "all of a sudden moment" of revelation of what was to be next.

Conception

I jolted from my bed, sat straight, and words came out of my mouth, "Yes, Lord, a women's conference." It was so straightforward and easy to understand.

My follow up question was, "Where, Lord?"

God was so clear, He simply said, "The Philippines. You will do something for the women first; after that, I will show you what is next."

I was confused on why it had to be the Philippines. Doing something this big in Manila felt dreadful and a bit alarming to me. Something inside my heart was being stirred up. Suddenly, all the painful things of the past came back to me. The rejection, the stigma of not fitting in, traditions and culture that brought painful memories, became so alive again in my heart as if I haven't left and lived out of the country for the last 27 years of my life. I was reminded of the norm of the society I grew up in. I did not realize that I still carried some baggage from the past. I had these traumas I wasn't even aware still existed. When I was growing up, fitting in meant you had to have a certain surname, go to certain schools, know someone powerful to help you, just to name a few. You had to be so connected to the leaders of the church, or they won't even listen to you. I felt disappointed that I relieved and entertained these thoughts about my past. This baggage had to be reopened, dealt with, and released. I needed to be healed. So, even before we went back to Manila, I asked the Lord to clean my heart completely and to lead me through the areas that needed to be completely healed.

Forgiveness is something I love to do because it clears out my head, lightens my heart, and helps me see Jesus and the situation I was in more clearly.

My prayer was, "Lord, help me. I truly want to obey, even if it is painful. I know You got it all figured out, Mighty God. I trust You, God". And so, with that, I gave God my "yes".

After our trips abroad, we headed to Manila, where we would wait for the next country that my husband's job would take him to. And I needed to start what God wanted me to do.

As soon as the plane touched down, the Beautiful Powerful Women Ministries was born.

Again, I had to begin from nothing.

I had not been in the Philippines continually for almost 3 decades, and so I had no one to rely on and nothing to start with. But I know my faithful and true God walks with me every single day. If He says so, the best way is His way.

Baby steps

As I was chatting with Daddy God, He reminded me of a group of people who invited me to speak twice in Manila. I met with them and told them the vision that God gave me, and in the beginning, they were all very supportive, excited, and promised to help. But slowly and surely, they all started leaving me right from the beginning till the middle of our planning. They just said, "Sorry, ate ('big sister' in Tagalog), we won't be able to help you and gave their reasons." It was heart-breaking, and as much as I wanted to self-check, I did not have the luxury of time to internalize. Although I felt every type of painful emotion I never thought I could feel, I knew I needed to walk past this, or over this, or through this, because I had a mandate to fulfill. It was a painful rejection, but I did not receive the vision from them, so I need to move on.

Side Note: I have learned that we truly have to put our trust in God, our eyes on Jesus and continually be reminded that by the power of the Holy Spirit, we have the ability to fight offense with forgiveness, and live in love and move on with or without the people you thought will be there for you.

God knows the right people that can help us to get His will done. More than anything, though, it is the journey that truly matters. How do we respond? How do we love in pain? How do we move on when we feel that people have abandoned us? We forgive and bless them and release them from our hearts and minds to the loving hands of Jesus and then move on because God will vindicate us in style. Our hearts, however, have to be focused on Him and not on vindication. But it's truly fun when God vindicates us. I won't deny that. Pure joy!

Going back to my story.

After the first team retracted their commitment, God allowed me to meet and be invited by a lady who hosts small gatherings with guests from outside of the country, and amazingly enough, with that gathering,I knew the people she invited from a few years back in Philadelphia. When it was time for prayers, they asked me to help pray for people during their ministry time. Some of the ladies that I prayed for were so wrecked by the love of God. I shared with them the vision God gave me. They showed interest in helping out and volunteered. We started meeting, and they became my new team. I had an amazing team who stayed with me till the end, and one of them is still with me. Her name is Janice.

Date and time

The very first Beautiful Powerful Women conference was scheduled for September 8. Incidentally, September 8 is celebrated in the Philippines as the birthday of Mary, mother of Jesus. I thought the timing was amazing. A double celebration! Since I was out of the Philippines for almost 27 years, there were so many things that I was not aware of about the country's holidays and traditions. I was so sure in my heart that the conference had to be on the 8th, so against all odds, I focused on holding the conference on that date.

I started looking for stadiums. Not a lot of people may believe me, but God is specific in giving instructions.

I felt like God wanted me to get a venue with a capacity for 8,000 to 10,000 people. I asked my team to help me scout for a place. We called and got connected to a lot of managers, but all of the places were fully booked due to the seasonal basketball games that hold at the same time. The last one venue we inquired in, however, said to us, "Oh yeah, please do it at our place, and we'll give you a discount." The manager said that the 8th was the only free date for the venue and they were very lenient with our down payment. Remember, I had no idea how this was going to be paid, but God knew. When the manager told me the amount of the required down payment, it was so reasonable, so I said, "I have that, let's book it."

Speakers trail

God is so detailed.

After I got the date and the place, I needed to decide who to invite as speakers. I needed the speakers to cover everything about what women are good at and more. I knew that I would have to meet people who would speak about healing, business, charity work, life coaching, beauty pageants, politics, and artists. Broad enough?

For healing

How I met this woman of God was fun.

My friend, whom I helped at the anti-human trafficking organization in Thailand, asked me to go with her to LA to attend a women's conference. It was there that I met Aunt Joan Hunter for the first time. I, somehow, ended up sitting around her after her session each day. Sometimes, I even bumped into her. On the last day of the conference, I found myself sitting behind her again, so she turned to me and said, "This is really something. There is something going on with our continuous meeting." I have been so captured by her simple and yet super powerful prayers in eradicating trauma and healing the sick. She had no exaggerations whatsoever. She just simply commands the sickness to go in Jesus' name and lays her hands on the person, and they are suddenly healed. She was a real supernatural woman of God. She sees healing and miracles happen all the time. When I met her, I didn't even know I was going to organize events yet, but she left such a mark in my heart that I knew she would be a great speaker, who would be able to impart what she carried to others. I invited her first to Thailand then to Manila to speak at the Beautiful Powerful Women (BPW) Conference. She agreed without hesitation. She is such a loving and amazing woman. To have her in my spiritual family is such a delight and a true blessing.

For charity work

I met Nancy Economou when she distributed solar-powered lights at the "Smokey Mountain" (a landfill, where a lot of people live) in Tondo, Manila. She is so precious and smart. On one of her trips to the Philippines, she saw a 13-year old girl whose face was burned by a kerosene lamp. As a mother, she felt that she had to do something. So, she prayed, and God gave her a brilliant design for a solar light that was perfect for the poorest of the poor in the remotest places around the world. This birthed her organization called Watts of Love, and she gave up her career for good. Since I have been traveling with her for years, I knew her heart. I knew how much she could contribute to the women, so I invited her to speak about her journey.

Business woman

The conference would not be complete without a representation of women in business. Teri Secrest is a very successful entrepreneur. Her joy in business was so strong it was captivating. I saw her from behind before she spoke at a conference in America. She was classy, full of grace, and she had a lot of creative ideas. When she finished preaching, I knew I had to have her someday. I met her again a few years later in Bali. She was with her daughter, Elizabeth, and I had the opportunity to invite them both to the conference. Teri was a motivational speaker for women in business, and Elizabeth agreed to co-host the conference with me. They were delightful mother and daughter tandem. It was powerful.

Life coach/author

I needed someone who is a young mother but also a leader. Aunt Joan said, "Take Charity." Meeting Charity Bradshaw was such a delight, and we had such a fun rapport. She is brilliant, so fun and lovely. She was also an author and a life coach. We felt so blessed having her in Beautiful Powerful Women. This woman of God is thorough, on point, and such a blessing to the women at the conference.

Locals

The roster of main speakers was complete, but deep inside, a voice was shouting, "You are doing this in the Philippines." So, this time, I thought, beauty queen, politician, and successful business owner must come from my own country.

I started to pray. Bring them to me, Lord.

Politician

This is fun. I truly believed that there should be someone to represent the government at the conference. I asked around because I felt that it was hard to find someone in the government who could say that they love Jesus, especially that they were in politics. A pastor told me to invite a certain Congresswoman, and I asked to be introduced. But it did not happen.

I prayed a simple and yet very effective prayer, "Lord, bring her to me."

One evening, I was invited by a local church for a local gathering. I came and was directed to the front row, where the Congresswoman was also sitting. "Ruth, this is the Congresswoman I told you about," the pastor said. I was overjoyed. I told her the story about how I had just asked God to bring her to me, so she had to be one of our guest speakers. Despite her busy schedule, she graced us with her presence. I love her because she is a woman who does not compromise. She was very sincere in her desire to defend the rights of the people, and she knew how to get her message across well. I was so happy that she agreed to come and share her powerful testimony at the conference.

Beauty queen

I was introduced to this lady through a church. As I got to know her more, I also learned that her life story was so powerful. From poverty, someone believed she had a destiny. So, despite the odds, she never gave up, but courageously lived her life. She was encouraged to joined a beauty pageant because she had the grace, the beauty, and the physique to be one. She didn't win the title, but her attitude was far from defeat. "We never lose, we just grow," she said. For that, she will always be a winner to me. I knew that she would be a blessing to many, and her perseverance will be such an encouragement to the women when they hear her speak.

Business owner

This lady knew how to evangelize! She is so on fire for the Word of God and wanted the Gospel to be spread all over the world. She uses every single platform she could to get the message across so that Jesus is introduced to the people. She was not there when I visited her office, but I witnessed how her staff would do their daily devotions and prayer time. They prayed every morning before work started. They were united in Jesus.

She had such a powerful story, as well. God gifted her with formulas of different kinds of herbal products that would enable people to get healed naturally without harmful chemicals from medicines. Her business succeeded tremendously while she was also becoming known for her knowledge, generosity, and love for God. I knew that I had to have her for the conference, and she graciously said yes. She was one who helped us the most. I honor her for all that she has done for BPW.

Entertainment

As Filipinos, we love to sing, and we loved gatherings filled with music. So, I thought it was good to feature talents from the entertainment industry, too.

My daughter was also starting out as a recording artist in Manila by this time, and through her, I met this amazing opera singer, whose mother was one of my daughter's voice coaches. She was happy to come and sing at the conference.

Through another artist friend, I met another singer, who happened to be the head of the orphanage I was visiting then in Manila. I asked her if she would come, and she also said yes.

NO worship, NO conference

Of course, I needed worship teams. One of our objectives for this conference was to help unite the body of Christ through worship. So, we invited some worship teams to worship and lead together with me. Jesus is worthy, so they said yes.

It was still a long process, but we were getting there.

God in us won't be denied

We were an unknown entity, but we were sent by the Lord. We needed to be seen, heard, and accepted so that everyone will enjoy what we have to offer. But how?

The businesswoman whom we invited to be a part of the conference gave us her full support. Glory to God, doors were opened to us – print, radio, TV. We were on page 2 of the second-largest newspaper company, we were in all top radio stations, including the secular ones, and Christian TV networks such as 700 Club Asia and TBN Asia, they all welcomed us. Other marketing opportunities became available, and 700 Club Asia opened its doors to us every year since. It was clearly God's favor. It was God.

It was so exciting because God's vindication was again so evident right before our eyes. When I asked for people to help us, some would say no, but all of a sudden, a door would open with the same but a bigger opportunity. The decision-makers and leaders would grant favors to us, and the people under them who declined us had no choice but to comply.

We put every need at the foot of Jesus, as we soaked in prayers and tears. We did what we could with all humility, using whatever we had, and God did not disappoint.

Almost none were buying the tickets.

Again, I soaked in prayers and tears.

It was a crazy ride.

In between all these preparations, I was also flying in and out of the country with my husband.

Flights, hotels, honorariums, food and many more

It is our joy to take good care of our speakers for the conferences and gatherings that we organize. We take care of their flights, hotel accommodations, and food. We want to bless them in the best way we could and honor them with a love gift.

I prayed about the provision for these things, since we were not advancing well in selling tickets. But God made it all work out at the end.

A month before the conference in Manila, I was invited to do a two-day worship conference in Hyderabad, India. We were in America for a month, and then we went to the Netherlands for a week, drove to Belgium for a night, flew to Thailand and stayed there for 11 hours, then went to Singapore and waited for 4 hours to catch the flight to Chennai. I was in Chennai for 11 hours and ministered in the streets while we were waiting for the flight to Hyderabad. By the time I arrived in Hyderabad, my body was so tired and beat that I completely lost my voice.

I prayed to Jesus, "You called me to be here; please bring my voice back." When I tried to speak, I could only squeak. I rested during the morning, and in the afternoons, I would have the worship band lay their hands on me and pray for healing. I kid you not; my voice was completely restored every evening at worship. The Holy Spirit was so tangible that our host church was so blessed. Hallelujah! On our last night there, the host asked me how much my travel expenses were on that particular trip. He reimbursed me for every single cent that I spent. Why am I telling you this? Because the amount he gave me was just right for the honorarium that was needed for all my guests. That was so exciting.

My take

The ride it took to prepare this conference seemed like a roller coaster, but on the day of the event, even though it was only a fourth of the seats that were taken, the sweet and tangible presence of the Holy Spirit filled out every space in the stadium.

Somebody came to me after and said, "I'm sorry that your show was not successful." I smiled in my heart and did not say anything because Jesus and I knew that first, this was not a show; second, Jesus was there; and third, the people who came were blessed and healed. They were already excited about the next conference. There were a lot of testimonies of healings and restorations from those who attended the event.

All the miracles, signs, and wonders that we experienced throughout this journey were truly irreplaceable. The Lord's teaching about humility and the price of obedience was something that we truly needed to learn.

The intense hurt and pain brought about by the opposition and oppression of the enemy through some people in the church did not discourage me. Disappointment of the numbers of attendees and other unexpected events that felt against us, all it did was intensely ignite the fire in my heart to be a platform of love, unity, and honor in the body of believers even more.

The speakers were all amazing and so loving.

I believed that no event I will do will ever be a failure.

I heard God all the way, and I did it the way I thought best.

I obey, and He brings in the people.

I still had three more to go, so I could not stop now. This was just the beginning.

I asked the Lord to cleanse me. I checked my heart and mind to ensure that every type of offense or pain was released and forgiven so that I could love afresh and bless the people who hurt me. And then, I moved on.

CHAPTER 8

BEAUTIFUL POWERFUL WOMEN 2: HEARTS ON FIRE

On to our next adventure.

This time, I felt that the Holy Spirit must be allowed to move, break barriers of religion, and let the fire and passion of His Love burn in the hearts of the people. Division and spirit of religion is so prevalent in the land so I felt like He wanted a platform that will allow Him to do as He please.

He alone can touch the people and transform them. We needed to invite His move, His ways, and His power to be manifested where we are, without boundaries, and get the nation fired up with holy love and passion for the One who is worthy. As we do that, we know that healing, joy, and unity will break out with no sweat. But at the same time , He gave me another revelation that I also needed to do in a smaller scale, He said specifically almost an audible voice, "bring the politicians to Me". I knew I needed to do two conferences.

I began to wonder however about the second mandate. My conversation went like, "Politicians, Lord? I don't know many of them, I only knew the president and the boxer senator, and surely, they wouldn't know me, they would probably not want to know me." But God asked me, anyway. It may sound weird or impossible, but He already knew that I would be writing a testimony of His amazing goodness. So, what do I do? OBEY!

WHO will speak?

I cannot personally think of any person who is filled with fearless passion, fire, and love of the Holy Spirit and lives in simplicity and great power like Papa David Hogan. He is like a father to me. He protects and loves me so well. We stayed in his house, and he is simply amazing inside and out. He prays for the dead, and the dead are raised to life. He lives the Word of God. He lives with great faith and love for family. He already has been my guest in Thailand, and we have already traveled together for missions in India, so it was easier to talk to him about speaking for Hearts on Fire. He said, "Yes".

Papa Mel Tari has a straightforward message about the Mighty Wind of the sweet Holy Spirit. He has such a fierce love for Jesus and an unwavering passion for the Gospel to be preached to the ends of the earth. He prayed for the water to be changed into wine, walked on very deep water, as if it was just knee-deep, and experienced many more miracles as he walked with the Holy Spirit. He focused on finding ways to make Jesus known. I grew close to him throughout the many conferences I joined with Heidi and Rolland Baker, and I have already previously invited him to Bangkok, and he also said yes.

Lastly, I needed someone from the Philippines, and I have always wanted to invite Pastor Hiram Pangilinan to speak. He has such a sweet and soft heart, he was like family to me, but more than that, he was a man of faith, anointed for miracles, healings, and revival. I love his passion for raising an army of believers to heal the sick in Jesus' name. He inspires every person who hears him to want to be a soldier for Jesus. The presence of the sweet Holy Spirit is undeniable in his life, and I saw how God worked in him in the many years of being friends with him. I knew that he needed to be one of the speakers from the Philippines. It was very special for him to finally meet Papa David Hogan. It was a glorious team-up. God is good all the time.

I always say, no worship, no conference. I invited two worship bands from two different churches. Practicing with them for worship was just soooo amazing.

Bringing the politicians to God

As I continued to walk along God's leading, His voice grew louder in my heart. I was not only to do a gathering for the Hearts on Fire in the astrodome, but also do a smaller gathering of politicians. I heard Him clearly say, "bring My politicians to Me!" It rang continuously in my ear.

As we walk with God, He will, sometimes, lead us to twists along our path to make it more exciting and challenging. When this happens to me, I know that it is meant to push me a little bit more to the supernatural, so that I can experience things that are not humanly possible. He continually asks me how much faith and how much I'm willing to risk for the sake of the Gospel. He just simply wants to show me more of Him.

I started to think and drain my brain about how to do the task at hand. Thank God, He reminded me that I can do things not by my own strength or wisdom, but by His leading, through the Holy Spirit[1]. I had to wait for a clearer direction from Him so that I could align my move with His vision.

God asked me to bring His politicians to Him. But it was election time, and politicians were busy, so I did not get any response from whoever was going to help me. It felt like I was facing a dead end. I was an unknown entity. Why would politicians want to come to a small gathering that I would organize?

But God is not an unknown, and He cannot be denied. So, I stepped out in faith.

I booked the 5-star hotel function room for the politicians' meeting. Then a month before the big conference, I started to feel so sad. "God, how do You want me to call Your people? How do You want me to lead them to come to us? I thought I heard you." My heart was sad, and I knew that it was because I was looking at what seemed to be the reality of my circumstances and not on Jesus.

I flew to Manila 4 weeks before the Hearts on Fire conference to do the last-minute preparations and promotions. When I arrived, I said, "Thank You, Daddy GOD, that it is You who asked us to do this, it is You who will make it all happen. Thank You, God, for

---

[1] Zechariah 4:8

inviting the people You appointed to come. I surrender to You and Your plans". These declarations reminded me of His promises and my authority to claim these promises, and it strengthened me. I was obedient in deed, but at that time, my heart was not obedient. God said, "Think of lovely, noble, beautiful, and praiseworthy thoughts.[2]"

But then, the most exciting thing happened. God made a way for me to meet President of the Philippines, and I was able to pray and prophesy over him. (I already explained this story in a previous chapter of this book.)

That was a pretty amazing thing that God did. Do you see how extravagant the Lord is when He wants to encourage us? Nobody in the world knew me, but I love God so much, and He loves and likes and knows me. I knew with all my heart that these favorable and victorious circumstances were orchestrated by God to encourage me. I have more of these stories, but that will be for another book. Before I arrived in Manila, I was almost complaining and demanding. When our hearts are so focused on what we think we need to see, we forget, and we doubt, and we complain. But He made a way when everything seemed impossible.

When God allowed me to meet the President, I became excited knowing that I was on the right track and that He is pleased and will see me through. I remember asking God, "Who will help me invite

---

[2] Philippians 4:8

the politicians?" And God answered, "Is there anyone higher in Philippine politics than the President?"

From then on, I did not care anymore if people would come or not. As long as I was sure that I was doing what God told me to do, I was on the right track, and the outcome of my obedience was placed in His hands. I obeyed until the end.

How did it go?

The meeting with the politicians we so powerful and yet relaxed. The main big one at the stadium, Hearts on Fire conference was truly an exhilarating and powerful experience with that was so full of His Tangible Presence. We all just did not want to stop worshipping, we were all so move by the His manifest Glory unexplainable, nobody wanted to go home. The focus was on God alone. It was so, so glorious. Everyone, I meant everyone. People from Mega churches who did not even believe in the touch and power the Holy Ghost left in awe and transformed. I could not wait for the next one. Oh, just remembering it, gives my heart such joy.

He knows us so well and is so patient and full of mercy. He is so gracious to us and gives us more than what we deserve. Nothing is really impossible with God. We need to be strong and continuously remind ourselves, in hope and faith, that He who called us is faithful, NO MATTER WHAT THE CIRCUMSTANCES BEFORE US MAY LOOK LIKE. He promised that He would be there for us, and so He is, and always will be there for you and me.

I am thankful that I did not give up. I thank God for His kindness, and I am awed that He still wants to partner with me. I love Daddy God so much.

As I always do after each event, I did a spiritual heart check, in case there is any unforgiveness or offenses that need to be released and forgiven so that I can continue to hear and see God clearly. Blessed by everything, time to move on.

CHAPTER 9
BEAUTIFUL POWERFUL WOMEN VIETNAM

I always believed that we should bloom wherever we are. There is always an assignment in the place where God puts us. So, although I was super busy with our Beautiful Powerful Women in Manila, I made sure that I heard from God, as well, about what I should be doing in Vietnam.

As soon as I arrived there, I felt a sense of urgency. I could not understand why I felt I needed to do things quickly. I even had the dates for a new conference ready. In the beginning, I worked with locals, but they have shown so much fear that I could not continue. God, however, is so good that He connected us to people who we could work with to get things done.

We previously lived in Hanoi for 6 years, and we still had friends there. Now, however, we were stationed in Ho Chi Minh. A family friend of ours found out that we lived in the same city, so he visited us and introduced us to other Filipinos who live in the same building. We had so much fun reminiscing the past. We also found out that the Filipino couple we met in the building were the same ones our friends in Manila wanted us to meet. God had it all figured out.

The couple were musically inclined and were really hungry for

God. We became so close, and we studied God's Word together. They knew my walk with the Lord. I told them the visions God placed in my heart for Vietnam, and they embraced it. They have been my help and support throughout.

There were three visions that God placed in my heart. A worship concert, a healing conference, and a ministry for women. While that was happening, I was also busy finishing a film project in the Philippines.

Thank You Lord Worship Concert

Barely three months in Ho Chi Minh city , I was already supposed to do this concert. I didn't know anyone because I was hardly there. I flew to Manila often for BPW, and I was also at the same time producing a film, so I really didn't know who could help me with this in Vietnam.

Since I am a worship leader, a songwriter, and an event organizer, I felt like I could do it without asking for someone popular to do the worship concert. The category for the worship concert was to have someone who loves the presence of God like I do or even more, I do someone who hosts the presence of God like I do or more, and someone who will invite the presence of the Heavenly hosts to Ho Chi Minh with passion like I do or more. I waited a bit for who can do it but no one came to mind or came to me, I said yes Lord , If none, I am willing. I had peace about the decision to just find a worship band that I could sing with, and it will all work out.

God was so amazing in orchestrating people. My neighbor's

church had a worship band. We did not need too much preparation; they only had to learn my songs. We also needed posters and other marketing materials that our team in Manila was kind enough to do for us. Our worship team was ready.

We needed to finalize the church venue. I asked permission from the pastor of my neighbor's church and invited them to collaborate. He knew my friends well, as they were the board members of the church. I felt that this was a perfect venue for our worship concert. It was such a favor from God. In about a month, we were able to do the concert, and not a lot of people came, but seven churches were represented in that event. It turned out to be a very prophetic event, and everyone wanted more.

A few months later, we set the motion to organize the healing conference. I had no second thoughts about who I was going to invite to speak. Aunt Joan Hunter was in my heart for this, and so I invited her. She came with her team. There were around 18 churches represented on that two-day training and hands-on healing conference. God showed up. It was a powerful conference and had some awesome supernatural manifestations of God's presence.

The Women's Conference was our last event.

We were in the Netherlands six months prior to our move to Vietnam. There I met my great sister friend Astrid from Holland. For the longest time, we have been exchanging ideas about how we could work together. She is the founder of Destined to Reign Ministries for women, and I felt that she would be the best fit to speak at a women's conference in Ho Chi Min. She has such powerful illustrations of how to reign as a child of the King and how to be loved and receive identity from God. The women's conference was so full of God's glory. Women truly encountered the Lord in that meeting.

Throughout the preparations in Vietnam, it was amazing how God stretched my time between conference and film premiere preparations in Manila as well.

I was in Manila for four full days to get the premiere of the movie done then I came back to Vietnam straight up for our conference. Both events were filled with His presence. These events were so miraculous, supernaturally transforming, and well-attended.

God is the master of our time. He can stretch it with no limits and shorten it anytime. He is sovereign. I love this, too, about Him. He is the God of Perfect Timing.

CHAPTER 10

BEAUTIFUL POWERFUL WOMEN 3: "HEARTS OF LOVE"

I felt that 2020 would surely be something unusual and will be a time where we will witness a brave move.

After Hearts on Fire, I already had two visions in my heart: encouraging people about missions – from home, with neighbors, overseas, or to the ends of the world; and clarity of visions for missions.

As a certified optometrist, 20/20 is significant to me because it meant perfect vision. It was so prophetic. God reminded me that as we give our testimonies in love and victory, they unlock many prison doors until the love and power of God can no longer be denied. As a testimony is shared, people will gain clarity and strength because they will see that they are not alone in the situation that they are in. It will empower them and bring revival.

The "brave move" in 2020 is the exposure of crucial situations being faced by our family members or our neighbors on a daily basis that nobody wants to address. Some things are just not easy to talk about.

The testimonies will bring clarity and understanding for the believers so that they can help the people around them who are hurting.

People need to see what is truly happening around and understand it well so that it can be addressed properly in love and toward love.

I would like to hear people say this after the Hearts of Love event: "I am already on a mission by the time I open my eyes."

Now that I understand better the situation around me, I can help address it wisely in Jesus' name. I have an order to receive the love of God and to spread that love and make God known. That is my mission.

But I have to be creative on how to execute these missions.

With God's help, "Hearts of Love 2020" was born.

Backtrack

At this specific point in our lives, while I was preparing for all these events, we were not sure if we would be moving to America from Vietnam. Nobody knew about all the commotion and tough decisions that my family had to make in the middle of all the decisions that had to be made, and the event preparations. We thought that our life was about to radically change because we would have to move again and probably stay permanently in one country. It was truly unusual, but we felt that this was God's biggest move for us. In all our 27 years of being married, the constant word for our family was 'change'. We moved all the time. The shortest time we stayed in one place was 4 months, and the longest was 6 years. God was so kind to have given us all these experiences; it was such a blessing to stay in the various countries we have lived in. It wasn't always easy, but it was fun.

This time, though, my heart was a little moved because I felt that moving to America would keep me far from all the ministries that the Lord established through me in Asia. So, one day, I finally asked the Lord if this was really His will; if I had to start agreeing with my husband about it. I asked the Lord if this is just one of those distractions. In my mind, I thought that it was not possible for us to go and stay in America for good, even if we travel there every year to visit my family. Also, I was too busy to even ask the Lord for personal stuff.

That day that I asked Daddy God, I was at the Thai Embassy in Vietnam to do some errands required for our American permits. As I crossed the street, I looked down, and I saw a dime on the ground. Okay, I was in Vietnam, in front of the Thai Embassy, and I felt there was a higher chance to find a coin in Thai Baht coin or Vietnamese Dong because the American Embassy was nowhere near and I didn't see any American tourists in the area. But God is so precise and intentional. He knows our language. Once He speaks, you will know it is Him. After that encounter, I knew I had to ask Him to change my heart and align my desires to His, to make it easier for me to obey. You will understand later why I had to tell you this story.

Back to the preparations of "Hearts of Love 2020".

Who is the epitome of a missionary? Someone who could give up everything, not quit, and stop for the one? My Mama, Heidi

Baker, of course. I needed to ask her, God was so clear on that.

No one can stop God's plan

I was supposed to meet Mama Heidi somewhere at a wedding, but somehow, it did not push through. I started wondering why, because deep in my heart, I knew she was supposed to be our next guest and conference speaker. I only had a few more months left to prepare, I just continued to pray that God would make a way for us to meet.

I went to Europe last October 2019 for my mother-in-laws' birthday celebration, and we were in Holland for less than two weeks. There was something heavy in my heart at that time that I needed help with. God is so sweet to make a way for me to see Mama Heidi whenever something major was going on in my life.

This time, though, I did not know at all whether I would be able to see her.

As soon as we arrived in the Netherlands, I heard from her former assistant that she was going to Frankfurt. This was the nearest place I could go to from where I was, so I asked my husband, and he drove me there. I spoke to her on the phone, and she said she would be happy to see me. So, I booked at the same hotel.

God knew I needed to meet Mama. We were able to talk about the conference over dinner, and it was set. I was doubly blessed because I met all her companions, too, and was encouraged by the prophetic words released to me by Brother Yun, the "Heavenly man" himself. It was a joy to meet him and his family.

Victorious love

I was looking forward to the sharing of testimonies about victory over abortion, drug addiction, promiscuity, and homosexuality. It was not meant to condemn anyone, but to strengthen the people and help them understand what happened in the lives of the people who struggled with it, but overcame, and are now living in victory through the love of Jesus Christ.

One day, I received an online call from a very good friend who told me that she felt like God wanted her to come again and join us at this event. It was a group call with her other friends who were also coming.

In our conversation, I told them clearly what God's vision was for this time. I didn't know them personally, so I had no idea about what their testimonies were. But as soon as I said that I wanted to expose the demonic giants that oppressed people, they volunteered to cover the very struggles we were targeting to deal with at the conference. One said, "I can cover abortion. I had a couple of them." Then our mutual friend said, "I can cover promiscuity. That was my lifestyle before Jesus changed me," and so on. Right after that conversation, my roster of speakers was complete. I didn't even ask for anyone; God just brought them to me, as I aligned with His heart.

It gives me so much joy to witness the miracles, signs, and wonders that follow us as we pursue the Holy Spirit and obey Him in seeking the lost. It does not get old.

I got everything ready.

We got everybody on board.

The place was secured and paid.

People and other organizations involved were ready.

And then COVID-19 showed up.

BackTrack

Remember when I told you we were moving?

Well, did I not also tell you that miracles, signs, and wonders would truly follow those that obey and love the Lord over and over and over ?

Within the year, and without waiting too long, we got our permits approved to move and live in America. That, in itself, was orchestrated by no one else but Jesus. However, that meant we had to move out of Vietnam three months before the Hearts of Love conference. I had to get ready for the biggest move of our lives.

It all went so fast, and I did not even realize it was already time for us to say goodbye to our friends in Vietnam. Closure is always a good thing. We bid our farewell, and off we went, not to the US yet.

We went to the Netherlands first to see our eldest daughter graduate from university with honors. God is truly merciful and so kind and so good. We knew that we would not be able to go to the Netherland for some time, so after celebrating my daughter's graduation, we stayed two weeks in my husband's hometown to spend time with my mother-in-law (my husband is so honoring and loving toward his mom). Then we finally flew to America, our new home.

We arrived in San Francisco, safely, in the first week of February. My entire family (parents and siblings) are Americans, so we felt at home there, but now, we had to adjust to being locals.

Back to Hearts of Love – a choice to make

Apparently, the process of getting a green card only starts upon arrival. That made me a little nervous because I was told I could not leave the country until after I get my green card, which would be around three months after our arrival in the USA.

To clarify, I knew that I just arrived, but after less than a month of arriving, I needed to leave again because the "Hearts of Love" conference would be held in March.

Things even got more eventful and complicated when the Covid-19 virus started to wreak havoc, spreading rapidly and caused a lot of fear all around.

By the second week of February, the height of confusion and doubt whether I could go to Manila or not was getting bigger and more challenging, day after day. To add to the pressure, my immediate family has now requested me not to go.

"Holy Spirit, what are You saying about all these?

All of a sudden, I wasn't sure.

Then the Holy Spirit asked me if I was willing to give up everything for Him. This will be the second time that He asked me about it.

The first time He asked me whether I was willing to give my husband and children to Him was when my kids were still very young. I could no longer remember the story, but I still remember the big revelation it brought me.

The more I get closer to God, the more I see me. The more I see me, the more I see my need to trust Him and entrust to Him, all the people I truly loved. The realization for me then was the same now, "I can't even love without the Lord. Why would I even have second thoughts about surrendering not only my family, but my all?" It is truly just about Him, in the end.

It is a kind of exchange. If I surrender them to the Lord, He can and will love them better than I could ever love them with my best.

A week before my flight, He asked me again.

"Will you give up everything for Me?"

I said, "Lord, there is no life, no future, no purpose, no joy without You. So, yes, I will give up everything for You again and again because You are trustworthy."

His nature is steadfast, and His name is LOVE.

He is faithful to His covenant, so I did not answer blindly. When I said yes to Him, it was with wholehearted hope and absolute trust in His mercy and loving-kindness. He is a good God. He will not withhold from me what is good for me .

"What is it that I have, Lord, that You have not given? Just say the Word, and I will obey."

A few more days had passed, and I still did not have my green card. We had also not heard from our lawyer. We went ahead and checked it ourselves and urgently. Finally, we were told that I was granted a temporary stamp of permanent residence on my passport, which was valid to use for travel.

Now, it's one thing to leave your family behind, and it's another thing not to be allowed back. This was a real worry because of the Covid-19 situation. I chose to believe that God will take care of me, and I would be allowed back. That brought me peace. I only now had to face the event in Manila and, of course, traveling in the middle of the ongoing pandemic.

Obedience is bigger than my fear, remember?

I heard the Holy Spirit loud and clear. He said, "go", so I told my husband. He knew I honored and loved him, so he needed to either say yes or no. I have been married to him for 27 years. We have a good understanding when faced with this kind of situation. He never stopped me, especially when he knows I have a go signal from Heaven; instead, he blesses and supports me in my decisions. I can't deny , this time it was harder for him than normal.

Early morning on the day I was about to leave, while still in bed, my sister rushed to my room and with great conviction, said, "don't go". A few minutes later, a friend of mine called me to say they were cancelling their flights and also discouraged me from going, or at least postpone my flight to a later day. At that point, my husband and our youngest child were already worried but could not tell me not to go.

My choice was made. Obedience is bigger than my fears. I needed to finish the work that the Lord led me to do. I knew that I could not back out.

I cried as they brought me to the airport. But I knew that I was doing the right thing. God's promises are real and trustworthy. I was sure that I would see my family again. It may be a wild ride, but it would be the right one.

I was asked to wait for 15 minutes at the exit counter while officers checked my passport to know whether I would be allowed back in. I bargained with God. "Lord, stop me, even now, if this is not You", I prayed. But right after I said that prayer, the lady came back and said that I was good to go, and God willing, I could come back.

I arrived in Manila, safe, and sound.

The real deal

Before I arrived in Manila, God already gave me a list of what I needed to do.

Help a church to encourage and strengthen them, their leaders and their members -- done! Visit a prison and sing to the prisoners -- done!

Go to the poor and minister in the area He specified -- done!

All of these happened within 10 days of my arrival, amidst all the meetings, prayer times, inner healings, speaking engagements, promotions, counseling sessions, not to mention the persecutions and the rising number of Covid-19 cases.

But as we obey, He makes us physically able and fit to complete the tasks at hand.

Our weaknesses are His forte. His strength is perfect for all of it.

I picked up Mama Heidi from the airport the night before the Hearts and Fire event was to be held, and that was when the big news was dropped: Metro Manila was to be quarantined.

I got a phone call from the team, and we were told that the venue we were going to use for the event had to be closed. President Duterte had just officially announced that all congregational meetings and activities are halted until further notice. Immediate action had to be taken because some of the officials at the event place had just tested positive for COVID. My head spun like a tornado.

My brother-in-law, who was with us in the car, also informed us of a possible lockdown that was to be implemented a few days after their meeting with the president.

Should I panic or just be at peace with Jesus? So many people were expecting and ready to attend the event. The two other churches organized events with Mama Heidi were also already prepared. But everything had to stop.

By the power and prompting of the Holy Spirit, I told Mama Heidi that we needed to tell the people that we were in Manila, we showed up, ready and willing to hold the events in the theater as promised, but we could not, due to reasons beyond our control. So it would become, instead, an online event, and things would happen as the Holy Spirit led. Mama Heidi agreed that this was the best thing to do. So, I called my team and made sure that our setup for a live telecast was prepared and ready for early morning the next day.

Finding a place to gather the team and hold the Facebook live announcement was another major challenge we had to face. The hotels now had to comply with the government's strict directive of social distancing. I started to pray differently.

Amazingly, a friend of mine called and suggested that I rent a presidential suite room. I checked out the room online. It looked like a television studio in itself. It was perfect. The cost did not matter. I booked the room, and we went straight there after a grueling three-hour journey from the airport.

Mama Heidi and I did an invite recording as soon as we got into the hotel room, then I asked my team to call the people we have made commitments to, as well. It was frenzy-crazy.

In a matter of 12 hours, the pandemic completely changed and disrupted everything we have planned and prepared for almost a year. It almost damaged relationships, too, but God is the Master Planner. The live Facebook event and podcast were powerfully executed, and we reached nearly 60,000 people that day instead of the

6,000 to 8,000 we would have reached in the theater had the event pushed through. Mama Heidi encouraged the body of Christ globally with such clarity and authority through the power of the Holy Spirit. She encouraged us to be the hands and feet of Jesus, that we were in a state of 911, and all hands must be on deck to lovingly help those we can help wherever we were during the challenging times ahead. It was the right message for everyone to hear at that particular time. What the enemy meant for evil, God used to reach more. That needed a Selah moment.

My flight home

As soon as the Facebook live and podcast was done, Mama Heidi, her assistant, and I worked to change our flights so that we could go back to the USA before the lockdown. I changed my flights so many times already and paid so much for all the changes, but this last change that would enable me to go home cost too much. I felt sad. I just could not get myself to pay for another ticket that was three times more expensive than the amount I already paid just a few days ago. I knew that the airlines had to make money, but charging so much during this kind of situation seemed almost inhumane. There were probably other reasons aside from the ticket that broke my heart, but I could not pinpoint why.

At the airport

I waited in the ticketing area at the airport for 8 hours altogether but I did not get the right ticket.

Everybody seemed to be panicking and didn't care about the high cost of air tickets. I, however, resolved not to let them take advantage of me anymore (or so I thought). I refused to buy another ticket from them. I was also very disappointed with how they made us, stranded passengers, wait forever without properly communicating with us. I felt that they didn't deserve my attention anymore.

I was tired. I had not slept properly for the last 2 weeks, and now this. I felt frustrated and still had no tickets. I was told that if I really needed to go that night, there was only one flight left. I had to decide. Thankfully, my super faithful assistant, Janice, accompanied me to the airport.

Japan Airlines was offering the only remaining flight that could leave that night. But Japan had a lot of bad COVID cases as far as I knew it. It was a crucial decision, but I needed to leave that night, so I took the risk and ended up paying just half the price of what the other airlines charged. As soon as it was done, I felt peace and was truly ready to go home.

It was a short flight from Manila to Japan, but the layover was 17 hours. I thought I could go out to meet my cousins, but my husband told me to stay inside the airport.

I thought, "Okay, let me just go to the airport's hotel to rest because I was really exhausted." But there weren't available rooms, and there was no way I could get out of the airport. With that, wrong thoughts circled my mind. I couldn't see the blessings anymore. I started to compare myself with others who could easily afford a flight. Out of frustration, it even crossed my mind that if I had not paid for the conference, I could have flown first class and would have arrived home by now. How shameful and arrogant my response was, and I knew there was no way I should even have this type of conversation with a sovereign, loving God.

So clear in my head, "So, you think you served Me so much already and gave up so much for Me?" Then He reminded me of what He did for me. He did not keep anything from me; He gave His Son for my sake. He gave His all—what a loving God we serve.

I repented of my arrogance and sense of entitlement. I repented for letting the exhaustion and stress get the better of me.

I believe fully in this truth: we have such an amazing, patient, loving God, who deals with us not as we deserve. He deserved my total devotion, honor, and adoration.

The 17 hours layover at the airport did me good in the end. I had a real talk with God about my heart, emotions, wounds, disappointments, and many other things.

You see, even as we are obedient to God, we sometimes also get into a discussion with Him, and He sets us straight every time, to improve us and grow us into His righteousness. Being a Christian does not mean that we can do everything right all the time, and we'll never be disappointed. We will, but we must move in humility, in the fear of the Lord and in true repentance, or we will completely miss it and waste our time.

In the end, my flight to San Francisco was easy and comfortable. As I came out of the airport, I felt clean, clear-headed, and filled with joy, hope, and victory. I happily saw my husband, who waited for me for 3 hours at the airport. We hugged and kissed, and finally, thankful to the Lord, we went home.

Some highlights again

The day after I arrived, the Philippine government announced a total lockdown, and a week later, we also had it here in San Francisco. Also, I received my green card the week after I arrived, then the US President said that no one else would be allowed to come into the country for a long time for any type of immigration. Moreover, two months after I arrived, the Beautiful Powerful Women Ministries Inc. was approved as a non-profit organization by the state of California. I was told that approval usually took 6 months to 2 years. And lastly, at least, for this book, three months after I arrived, I was ordained as a pastor. Now, these are all only Jesus.

The perks of obedience are miracles, signs, and wonders. We truly get to walk and enjoy it every step of the way.

He alone deserves all the glory, all the honor, and all praise.

A new season, a new chapter is again ready to begin.

CHAPTER 11

A BONUS STORY

I should probably not write this one now, but I feel truly led to do so.

First event in the US was such a history

BackTrack

During my husband's sabbatical time, it gave us both some time to really ask God where He would have us enjoy our promised land on earth. But more than that, we wanted to know where we would go now that we are getting older, and the kids are grown up.

All these years, we had lived such a blessed life, traveling around the world. At some point, we really had to start praying to God for direction. We knew, of course, that our immeasurable, powerful, glorious God had the best plan for our lives. He brought us to places where we actually wanted to be, as well. God is so sweet to answer our secret desires.

Now, God brought us to America, where we will be permanently living in. Only God can do this. I choose to enjoy Jesus here one day at a time. During my first three months here, I often prayed while walking around and listening to Him. I just enjoyed the loving presence of Jesus.

He told me that the first project He wanted me to do was all about women -- to empower, revive, and restore them. God told me to gather women ministers and leaders from around the world who will be able to meet online to pray, love, prophesy, and minister over one another.

With God's help, I was able to connect with the women leaders here. Thankfully, they are able to work with me on this project.

As God continued to connect me with the women here, I also started calling people I knew from around the world that I felt God wanted me to touch for this project. My desire was to pull in leaders who can truly express love and understanding to the women that will come to us through God's leading.

After talking to a lot of the prominent ministers and leaders, I asked the Lord for somebody who can help me with the technology needed, and God brought her to me. She knew exactly what to do for the work that needed to be done.

In the beginning, it did not seem like I had enough women to minister, so I started tagging leaders who could bring along other leaders into the ministry. We had such an amazing connection, and the group grew through what seemed to be a powerful Kingdom multiplication process.

The initial meeting was on fire!

The women were so focused on each other. The leaders were so humble and yet so supernaturally powerful. The love of God, the most important factor, radiated to each other across the boundaries of distance and time.

We had 50 ministers literally from around the world, ministering to 70 other women together in one zoom gathering, all at the same time . It was so glorious. The simplicity, inclusivity, unity, honor, and love that we wanted to give the women were exquisitely accomplished.

We are set to do this three months in a row. This is what God told me, and I am just joyfully obeying. Again , Im new here , did not know anyone but at the end ,He brought the people I needed.

You see, we get to enjoy the ups and learn lessons during the low points.

We really just need always be connected to Jesus. He is the one who gives the visions, the instructions, the people, the provisions, and the strategies for the right implementation.

At the end of the day, it is all about His ideas , His purposes and His dreams for us.

Ours is our obedience.

CHAPTER 12
HOW ABOUT YOU ?

This is mine:

Jesus introduced Himself to me and captured my heart and gave me a new life.

A love story with Him began.

A love story that has been exciting and adventurous, on a daily basis.

He continues to take me deeper in His love and causes me to understand His heartbeat.

He shows me great and amazing things beyond my imagination.

My love for Him explodes within me; I can't contain it.

His love for me and my love for Him encourages me to be a part of what He does every single time.

I am so full of life within me. I have decided to be His, for the rest of my life.

God:

Whoever loves Me, obeys Me.

Me:

I will obey, Lord, help me.

God:

I am with you and will walk with you all the days of your life.

Me:

I choose that walk.

How about you?

My first question might have to be, "How is your love story with the Lord?"

Has it been so intense that passion is born? Passion to partner with Him in wanting others to know His love, too?

How is your yield like lately?

Have you been so busy that you have no time to listen to Him? That instead of obeying, you do things you think He wants you to do, rather than truly hear Him first and do what He wants you to do?

Don't be deceived. It is better to obey than sacrifice your time and energy. Obedience has lasting fruit, but sacrificing outside of God's will, will just wear you down. [3]

Do you lack vision lately?

You can always stop and step back for a while. Pray! Let's go back to Him. Make Him first in our lives again. Even now, you can

---

[3] 1 Samuel 15:22-24 TPT

ask Him to make you a partner of His move again. I love that He gives new beginnings. Now is a good start.

Do you have a dream with God now?

What keeps you from doing it and moving with it?

How we think either helps us move or not. If we think the task is too big and we can't do it, that is the best opportunity to stretch and increase our faith. God promised in the book of Matthew that "nothing is impossible with him that believes."

Remember to ask for and look out for the miracles that are supposed to be following you and the immeasurable favors that are already prepared for you.

In case you don't have dreams right now, this you can now declare:

"Awaken Your Dreams, Lord, within me, that's my prayer right this minute. I say yes to partner with You to fulfill it. In Jesus' name. Amen."

Is Faith or Fear tricking you?

Like Peter, he started to walk on water but started to sink as fear beset him when he saw his surroundings[4]. But Jesus was there, and pulled him up again and got him back to safety.

Fear looks like, "You can't" and "It won't work", but faith says, "It's been done and paid for on the cross. I just have to walk through

---

[4] Matthew 14:22-33 TPT

it, and God is here with me all the way."

The good He started in us, He will finish in greatness. Obedience defeats fear because faith says, "With God all things are possible".[5]

Are we in line with God in how we execute our calling?

How about feeling stuck?

No one will ever be stuck when the Lord is with him. He is a God of movement, revelation, and increase.

It is often our past or present experiences that tell us things can't be done. Our minds can play tricks on us. We have no excuse because our God is a life-giver, full of adventure and excellence.

Say NO to delayed obedience because delayed obedience is disobedience.

We do not want to be disobedient. It keeps us far from God's radar and away from His presence. When His presence is not there, His blessings are not there, too.

Without God's presence, there is no life.

How about feeling belittled, unaccepted, and opposed by people, disappointed, frustrated, and dishonored?

You read how I felt it every single time I did something new. As long as you are doing something good and different, and from God,

---

[5] Matthew 19:26 TPT

there will be opposing forces. The enemy will stir up people to discourage, hurt, and even destroy you. That is the devil's scheme.

But I have a regimen for this: forgiveness. We must resist offense and keep our hearts clean before the Lord. You might say it is so hypocritical. The thing is, I did not say you won't feel hurt, betrayed, offended, angry, and so on, but what I am saying is, don't stay there!

We give it all to the Lord, and He will help us deal with it.

This is crucial because when our hearts are not right, the way we perceive things also gets distorted. We do not want that. We have to go to God because we can do nothing without Him. With Him, all things work out, and the impossible becomes possible because what is impossible does not exist for Him.

We are called for a purpose.

We are all uniquely designed to do the good works God has predestined for us to do[6].

We all have our gifts and assignments.

We are all brilliant in Jesus.

---

[6] Ephesians 2:10

There is no more excuse not to obey. His love casts out all our fears so we have the courage and ability to not be afraid to do what He asks of us. But more than anything, obeying Him is such honor.

Let's just go back again to the beginning. "Love God and be passionate about Him." Seek Him and want more of Him. This will automatically cause you to want to obey Him. It does not mean, you will. But wow, with a trustworthy God likes ours, so merciful and patient and only think of what is best for us, it is more of a privilege to do so than not.

My chosen lifestyle is OBEDIENCE .

How about you ?

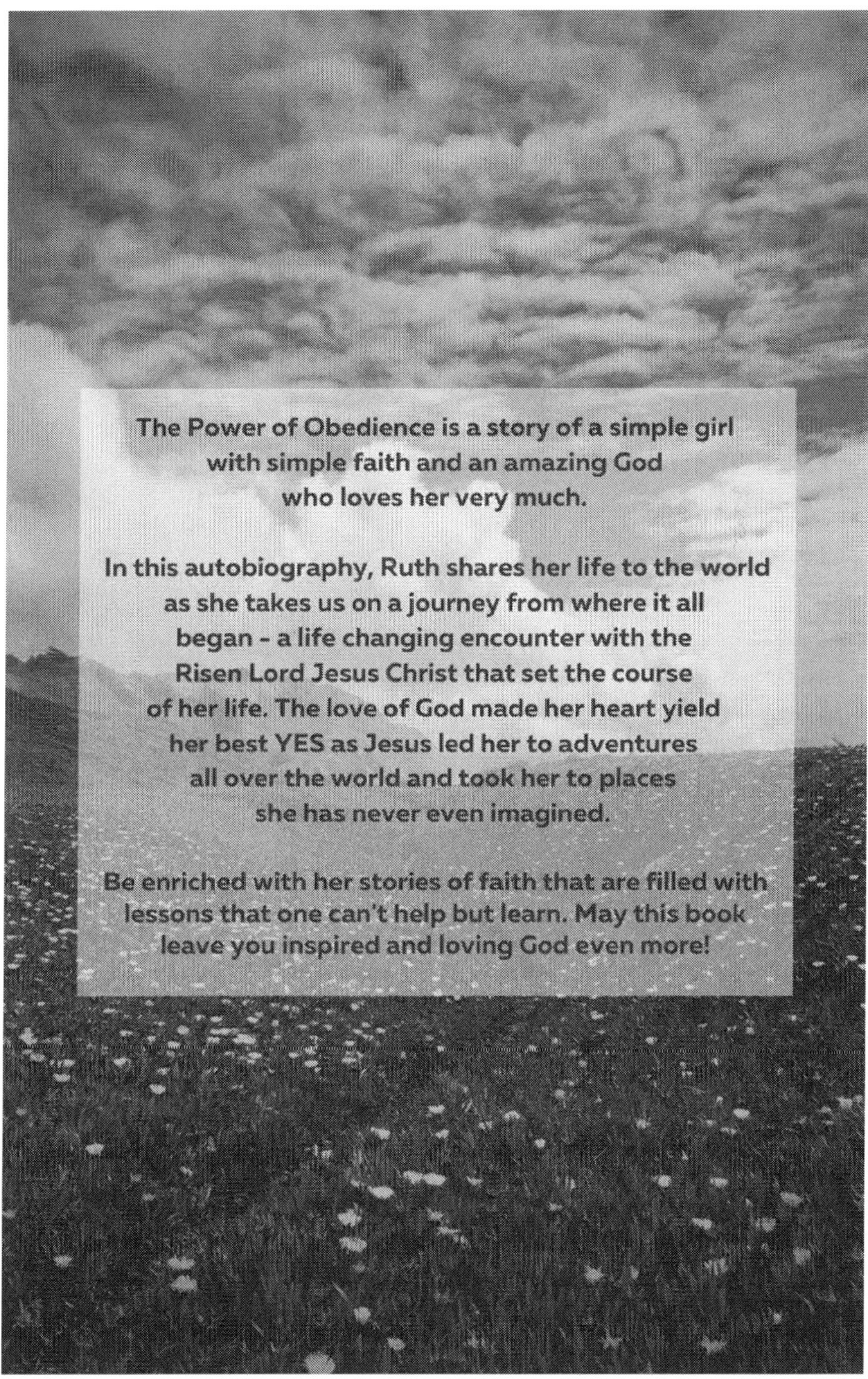
The Power of Obedience is a story of a simple girl
with simple faith and an amazing God
who loves her very much.
In this autobiography, Ruth shares her life to the world
as she takes us on a journey from where it all
began - a life changing encounter with the
Risen Lord Jesus Christ that set the course
of her life. The love of God made her heart yield
her best YES as Jesus led her to adventures
all over the world and took her to places
she has never even imagined.
Be enriched with her stories of faith that are filled with
lessons that one can't help but learn. May this book
leave you inspired and loving God even more!

Printed in Great Britain
by Amazon